A WITCH'S GUIDE TO MURDER

A BOOK & CANDLE MYSTERY BOOK ONE

AUBREY HARPER

A Book & Candle Mystery

A Witch's Guide to Murder

A Witch's Guide to Werewolves

A Witch's Guide to Hauntings

A Witch's Guide to Vampires

A Witch's Guide to Familiars

A Ghost Hunter P.I. Mystery

Ghostly Apparitions

ONE

"C'mon, it'll be fun!" I said to my best friend Scott, trying to convince him to come with me to my grandmother's funeral.

You might think that was a bit odd, but both Scott and I were struggling. He was a copyeditor who really wanted to be a mystery writer and I was a waitress in a crappy diner who really wanted to be an actress.

We lived in New York. Not the city, just the state, and when I heard that my grandmother died and possibly left me everything, I jumped at the chance. But Scott didn't seem to be having any of it.

"I don't know, Rory," he said, looking like he wanted to be anywhere else but where he was. I ran my hands through his dirty blond and always messy hair.

"It's gonna be fun!"

"It's a freaking funeral, how fun can it be? Plus, I

can't call off work and you know it."

"That place is working you to your bones. This is a sign, Scott!"

"A sign of what exactly? That you didn't like your grandmother very much? You seem awfully chipper about the whole thing."

I rolled my eyes. "You know it's not like that. I barely even knew the woman. My mother made sure of that." It was a long story, but the short version was that mother never liked my grandmother and she forbade me from even speaking to her.

I tugged at the heart necklace I always wore. It was the only thing that my grandmother ever gave me and my mother reluctantly let me keep.

"Besides," I continued. "This will be the perfect opportunity for you to work on your book. The lawyer said that she pretty much left me everything. Her shop, her house, and God knows what else. You can work on your writing, help me around the shop, and live with me! It doesn't get any better than that."

Scott groaned. "Fine. I'll go with you to the funeral, but that's all I'm promising."

I jumped up with joy and ran to my room to retrieve the plane tickets. I lifted them up in the air.

Scott sighed. "You know me better than I know myself, don't you?"

"Of course, silly."

Scott put down the boring stuff he was copyediting.

"I guess I'll have to call my boss and hope he gives me some time off."

"Family emergency. Death in the family. He can't fire you for that!"

It was Scott's turn to roll his eyes. "I don't know why you're so excited about this. Didn't you say that Hazelville was the most boring place on earth and that you couldn't wait until you got away? And now here you are all excited about going back."

I breathed in hard. "That was before. But now that I know New York isn't as glamorous as it sounded, I'm ready for a change. What's so wrong with that?"

"Nothing, I guess," Scott admitted.

The rest of the night was spent packing. Thankfully, black was my favorite color so I didn't have much trouble packing a few funeral-ready attires.

I looked at myself in the mirror. Hazel eyes and shoulder-length black hair stared back at me. Of course, I dyed my hair black. It was naturally light brown.

You might think I'm some kind of goth, but the truth was that I just preferred black over any other color. It looked the best on me.

I tugged at the heart necklace again and thought about how it was the only connection I had to my grandmother.

"I'm sorry granny," I said instinctively. "I'm sorry I never really knew you."

"YOUR GRANDMOTHER WAS A WITCH, wasn't she?" The cabbie said as he drove us to my grandmother's shop, Book & Candle.

"Yes, at least that's what they tell me. I never put much stock into those stories," I said and tried to brush off his comment. Scott had his head in a book, though I could see that he was really listening to our conversation. I never told him about how my grandmother was known as the local witch.

"I didn't mean anything bad by it. God knows I've driven my wife to your granny's shop more than on one occasion," the cabbie said as he continued to look straight ahead.

I breathed a sigh of relief. When people talked about witches, especially people in Hazelville, Ohio, they didn't really speak of them in positive terms.

"Now, I don't believe any of that mumbo-jumbo," the cabbie added when he realized I wasn't going to say anything. "But it keeps the wife happy, so what can I say?"

I smiled at him.

"You're a smarter man than most," I said and saw Scott roll his eyes at me. The cabbie laughed.

"Here we are," the cabbie said as he parked right in front of my grandmother's shop. Book & Candle. It looked quite different than I'd imagined.

"Thank you for the ride, kind sir," I said as I handed him the cab fare.

"See you around Ms. Wiltz!"

With that, the cabbie drove off.

Scott and I stood by the curb with our luggage.

"Was that the best idea?" Scott asked. "I mean letting the cabbie go. How will we get to a hotel?"

"Scott, you worry too much. We'll just call ourselves another cab, okay?"

Scott rolled his eyes. He followed me into my grandmother's shop. It was open and there was a young woman behind the counter. She looked vaguely familiar but I couldn't quite place where I'd known her from.

There were no customers in the shop, which wasn't a good sign for me, especially if I was to be the new owner.

When the girl behind the counter saw me her face lit up. Then she saw the luggage I was carrying and realized who I was.

"Rory? Is that you?" The young woman said. She was probably in her early twenties and had long curly brown hair and dark brown eyes. Scott and I were in our late twenties, and I already found myself envious of her. The older I got, the more I resented those younger than me.

"I'm Rhi! Your cousin. Remember we used to play as little kids?"

As a matter of fact, I did not remember, but I nodded politely anyway. "Yeah, Rhiannon, isn't it?" Thankfully, I did remember her name.

"That's right! This is so exciting!" She said as she gave me a generous hug. I nearly dropped the luggage and eventually just let go of it and hugged her back. "I mean, not about granny dying, but about you coming back to town! I remember I heard you said you'd never step foot here again last time we spoke."

"Yeah, the foolishness of youth and all that," I said and tried to brush the past away. I wasn't really in a reminiscing mood. I was here to find out what my grandmother left me and how much it was worth.

In that spirit, I took a good look around the shop. Candles, herbs, crystals, spell kits, and a generous collection of books.

"It's amazing, isn't it?" Rhi offered and I smiled back at her.

"It's something," I said. "But it doesn't seem to be too busy..."

"Yeah," Rhi agreed with a sad look on her face. "It's been pretty slow the past few years. Thankfully, the online sales have more than picked up the slack."

"That's great," I said. "Isn't it, Scott?"

Scott still had his head in a book. An Agatha Christie novel if I wasn't mistaken.

"Wow! You're a mystery fan?" Rhi asked Scott and he nodded.

"He wants to be a mystery writer," I added and Scott looked about ready to kill me. He hated when I told people about his writing.

"There's a bookshop right across from here. Booked for Murder. It sounds right up your alley, Scott!"

Scott's mood brightened up a little. "I think I'll go check it out. Can I leave my luggage here for now?"

Rhi nodded. "It's fine. Just put it behind the counter."

Once Scott was out the door, I was left by myself with the ever-bubbly Rhi.

"C'mon, cousin. I'll show you the back room."

I looked at the empty shop. "What if a customer comes in?"

Rhi looked at me like I'd said something terribly ridiculous. "There's a bell above the door. We'll hear if anybody decides to drop by."

I followed her to the back room. There were boxes strewn around everywhere, but there was a table in the middle with a computer. She moved the mouse and the screen came to life.

She showed me the shop's site. Book & Candle: For all your Occult Needs, it said.

"As I said, most of our business is online. I guess people don't want to be seen entering our shop. At least not in this town."

I had to agree with her there. Hazelville was a small town where gossip traveled fast. I wasn't one to care much what other people thought of me, and I still felt a little on edge being there.

"How long have you worked here?" I asked Rhi.

"About two years full-time. Used to be part-time while I was in high school."

I walked around the back room and noticed stairs leading up to the attic.

"I wonder what's up there?" I asked my cousin.

"Oh, that's granny's secret room. No one was allowed up there. Even I don't have a key."

"Oh, that's strange," I said, though I wasn't really sure why.

"You have an appointment with the lawyer tomorrow, don't you?" Rhi asked. "Maybe she left the key to you." I could see that Rhi was trying to stay neutral as she said those words, but I could also see that she was slightly disappointed that our grandmother seemed to have left everything to me, her oldest granddaughter.

"So what really happened to her?" I said, trying to change the subject. I definitely wasn't in town to stir up any family drama.

"It's sad. She actually died right here. They found her at the bottom of these stairs. The cops say it was an accident, but I have other ideas." For the first time, Rhi looked really sad about the whole ordeal.

"Why do you think it wasn't an accident?"

"It's just a feeling. Call it intuition if you will," she said and gave me a knowing look.

I wasn't quite sure if I was supposed to know what she was talking about. Was she trying to tell me that she was psychic somehow?

"Anyway, you probably want to crash after such a long trip, don't you?" Rhi said and thankfully changed the subject. I wasn't quite sure what to say to her little theory about our grandmother's death not being an accident. Surely the police would know better than a twenty-year-old girl?

"Is there a motel or Inn close to here?"

"That's silly. Gran's house is practically yours already. You should crash there," she said as she looked through a bowl of keys and other trinkets. "Ah! Here they are," she said as she handed me the house keys.

"Thanks," I said. It felt strange to hold the keys to my new house. "Now all I need is to call a cab and Scott and I will be on our way."

"Don't be silly, cousin Rory! I'll give you guys a ride," she said as we walked out to the main part of the shop. "This place is dead anyway. I doubt anybody will miss me for half an hour or so."

Rhi helped me put the luggage outside. I went and fetched Scott, who was in an aisle full of Agatha Christie's.

"This place is awesome," he said and I just rolled my eyes.

"Is it just as you remember?" Rhi asked me as we drove to my grandmother's place. I looked at my surroundings and wasn't really sure what to make of any of it. Small shops. Small houses. Just a tiny town I never thought I'd step foot into again after my mother moved us out.

"I guess," I said.

"Yeah, nothing much changes around here. You don't know how jealous I was when I learned you'd moved to New York, but of course, my mother forbade me to step a foot outside Hazelville."

"I wonder why that is?" I mused out loud. "My mother is the only one from the family that I remember ever moving out of here."

"Old habits die hard I guess," Rhi said and laughed nervously. I knew there was something she wasn't telling me, but I wasn't so sure I wanted to find out what it was just yet.

Rhi stopped in front of a Victorian-like house. It looked like it'd been there quite a while.

"Wow, I forgot how beautiful this house is," I said and meant every word. I was in awe of it as I stood on the curb and waited for Scott to join me with our luggage.

Rhi smiled. "It's always been my favorite place to hang out," she said. "Well, see you around cousin!"

I waved goodbye to her and actually found myself liking her right then and there.

Scott looked up at the old Victorian and made one of his faces.

"Spooky," was all he said as we made our way up to the front door.

TWO

IT FELT STRANGE TO BE INSIDE THE HOUSE OF SOMEONE who was dead. I remembered what Rhi had said about our grandmother's death not being an accident, and I quickly locked the door behind me.

Scott put down our luggage by the door; he looked exhausted. He wasn't used to heavy labor and I couldn't blame him.

"Water," was all he said as I walked around until I remembered the general area where the kitchen was.

"Here it is!" I said excitedly as I walked around the big kitchen. There was a big fridge in the corner which I immediately opened.

There was a bunch of foil-wrapped food. Probably brought in by people who'd heard about my grandmother's sudden death.

"I'm not eating anything that's not sealed by the

manufacturer," Scott said as he rummaged the fridge for some water. He found an unopened can of Sprite instead and drank it before I could utter a word. "We should probably go shopping soon. You know tap water isn't good for you."

I nodded. I certainly agreed with him there. I took a can of Sprite myself and drank some. The cold carbonated drink felt refreshing going down my throat.

"This place is pretty big," Scott observed as we walked into the spacious living room, which was furnished in all things antique. Even the bookshelves were filled with books that looked like they belonged in another century.

The huge, glass-stained windows all around were my favorite feature of the house.

"It sure is. I still can't believe she left everything to me. I won't believe it until I speak to the lawyer tomorrow. It all seems like a misunderstanding. She barely even knew me."

After we got our energy back, our next task was finding rooms. Finding a room for Scott wasn't much trouble. He got the room that looked the barest and used the least, probably a guest room. He seemed happy enough with the arrangement because he immediately started unpacking a few of his things.

I, on the other hand, could not make up my mind where to park my things. I walked around randomly until I reached a big imposing door that I remembered from when I was a kid.

This was definitely my grandmother's room. I wondered what I would find behind that big scary door.

I turned the handle and was surprised to find the room unlocked. The first thing I noticed was the altar in the corner of the bedroom. An assortment of half-burned candles and other witchy items were placed there in a seemingly random order. I saw a piece of paper with some strange symbols on it.

I sensed movement in the room. I sighed in relief when I saw that it was just a cat. It was sleeping in the middle of the bed and blended in with the dark covers.

"Scott, look what I found!" I yelled out and Scott soon joined me.

"Here, kitty, kitty," I said as I started to pet the creature. At first, I thought it was all-black, but soon it became apparent that there was a shade of blue there as well. "You're quite unique, aren't you?" I said as I petted it.

The cat didn't pay much attention to me. It just kept on napping.

"I love cats," Scott said as he reached out to pet the creature himself.

The cat hissed and almost managed to scratch him.

"Ouch! Well, that wasn't very nice, now, was it?"

"It doesn't seem to mind me..." I said fiendishly.

"Yeah, yeah. Whatever," Scott said and then noticed

the altar in the corner. "So your grandmother was really into this stuff, wasn't she?"

"I guess so," I said.

The rest of the day was spent going out and shopping and filling our fridge with bottles of water, some fresh food, and other stuff we needed. The same cabbie who'd given us a ride to Hazelville gave us a ride this time. He said that only he and another man worked in the area.

When we got back home the cat was still there in my grandmother's bedroom.

Later that night I found myself walking in the house. I had no idea where Scott was, but he was probably back in his bedroom.

"Follow me," I heard a familiar voice say. I followed the sound of the voice until I was inside my grandmother's bedroom. I was at her altar and I was looking down at the candles which were lit now. I wasn't really sure what I was doing there. Earlier that day I had chosen another bedroom because it just seemed too creepy to sleep in the bedroom of a dead person.

A sense of knowing washed over me as I approached the altar. I put my hand at the locket around my neck and felt the heat coming off of it. I heard a voice in my head say that I should open the locket and I did so. Something strange started to happen, but I wasn't really sure what exactly.

Strange words echoed inside my mind, and then in

English, they kept saying that I should repeat the words. I did as I was told, even though I wasn't sure if this was the right thing to do.

I said the words and a powerful feeling washed over me. I immediately let go of the locket as a figure appeared in the corner of the room. I jumped up from the fright and just as I did I woke up in my bed sweating, as close to screaming as I have ever gotten in my life. But somehow I knew to keep quiet.

I looked at the corner of the room where a figure appeared in my dream and saw another figure there now. It was an older lady who looked exactly like my grandmother.

"It took you long enough," she said.

I OPENED MY EYES. I closed my eyes. She was still there.

"Stop acting silly, Rory. It's your grandmother Rose. Don't you recognize me?" my grandmother said.

"This is impossible, this isn't real," I kept repeating to myself while closing and opening my eyes, trying to make the figure of my dead grandmother disappear.

"Rory, I thought you were smarter than this," my grandmother said as she looked at me sternly. She walked around the room, and even though she was see-through, she seemed more solid than even I.

Maybe I was still dreaming? Maybe this was all just a crazy hallucination? I tried to convince myself of that fact and even pinched myself and almost screamed out from the pain. But my dead grandmother was still there walking around like it was nothing.

"Rory, get a hold of yourself, girl," Rose said as she stood right in front of me.

"How is this possible?" I said as I ran my fingers through my hair in frustration. "You're supposed to be dead!"

"Dead? Of course I'm dead, you silly girl."

"Then why are you here?"

"Well, you just did a little spell so you could see me," she said. Then she smiled a smile that sent shivers down my spine. I didn't know what to think of any of this. Was I going crazy? Was this really happening?

"Rory, I have something to tell you."

"What is it, grandmother?"

"You're a witch, I'm a witch, and there's nothing you can do about it."

"How is this even possible? I thought all this witch stuff was mumbo-jumbo? And you're telling me this stuff is actually real? I mean, I know that people do spells and stuff, but I never thought it actually worked like this. I thought it was just the power of positive thinking."

"Silly, silly girl. Those people know nothing about real magic or real witchcraft. I'm here to show you what a real witch can do," she said as she basically walked through a dresser.

"And how are you going to do that?"

"I'm doing it as we speak, my dear granddaughter."

"But why are you doing any of this? Was your death really an accident or was it murder like Rhi said?"

"Unfortunately, your cousin is right. I was murdered, but I don't know by whom."

"How could you not know? Aren't you a witch? Doesn't that mean that you would know who killed you?"

"You would think so, wouldn't you? But yes, you are right about one thing. I should know who killed me. If it was a regular person, a mundane as we say in the magical community, I would have known who had done this to me. But the sad truth is, I have no memory of what happened that day. I just know I woke up and I was a ghost. I knew I was dead, of course. Witches always know. But, I did not know who was responsible."

"What are you trying to say?"

"I'm trying to tell you that my death was not an accident. Another witch was responsible."

This was all a bit too much for me. I wasn't even sure I believed in any of this witch stuff, and here was my grandmother telling me that she was murdered by another witch. How was that even possible? And even if it was, I didn't know what she wanted me to do about it.

"I want you to solve my murder, silly! That is the only way I will find my peace, if I actually know who put me in this state. It might not seem like it to you, but I had plenty to live for!"

I rolled my eyes. Was my grandmother actually serious about me solving her murder? I wasn't a cop or a detective.

"Where are you going?" Rose asked as she saw me exiting the room.

"I'm going to wake up my friend, Scott," I said as I made my way to his bedroom.

To her credit, my grandmother followed me all the way there. I knocked on the door and then basically opened it myself.

As usual, Scott was in bed reading a paperback.

"Knock much?" Scott said as he put his book down.

"Do you see anyone behind me?" I pointed to my grandmother who was standing right behind me with a huge grin on her face.

"What the hell are you talking about? Did you have too much to drink or something?" Scott looked at me like I was crazy.

"Of course he doesn't see me, he's not a witch!" My grandmother said as if it was the most normal thing in the world.

"And I am?"

"Who are you talking to?" Scott seemed really concerned for my sanity right then and there, and I can't say I blamed him. If he started to talk to nobody in the middle of our conversations, I would think he was crazy, too.

"This is crazy, I can't believe this is happening to me," I said as I once again ran my fingers through my hair. How was this even possible?

"Well, he would be able to see me, if I wanted him to," my grandmother said with a mischievous look on her face.

"So, why don't you do that?"

"Who are you talking to? Why are you acting like this?" Scott seemed really concerned for me. He was a good friend, after all.

"Once I do this, there is no going back. Us witches have hidden ourselves for centuries. For fear of persecution, fear of death, and things much worse than that."

"Oh really? Everyone in town knew you were a witch!"

"They didn't *know* I was a witch, they thought I was a crazy old lady who thought I was a witch. There's a huge difference, as you should know better than anyone, my dear sweet Rory."

"This is getting frustrating," I said more to myself than either to my grandmother or to Scott.

"Rory, maybe you should go back to sleep," Scott looked more concerned than ever. I had a feeling he was thinking of calling for help, but he thought better of it. He knew I would kick his ass if he told anybody about me acting crazy.

"Let's go somewhere private and continue this conversation because I really have no time for this," Rose said. She crossed her arms across her chest, which was a strange sight since she was completely see-through.

"Scott, get up, get dressed, and follow me," I said as I went downstairs to the living room.

My grandmother followed me, of course. I sat down on the sofa and waited for Scott to arrive as well. We were going to get this settled once and for all.

THREE

"Here comes the fruitcake," my grandmother said in a whimsical voice.

I snickered despite myself as I saw Scott coming down the stairs. He joined us, with a perplexed look on his face.

"Am I missing something here?" Scott stood in the middle of the living room looking at me like I was crazy.

"Sorry, it was just something my grandmother said."

"You *are* crazy, aren't you?" Scott said as he crossed his arms just like my grandmother had earlier, but thankfully he looked normal.

"If you want this fellow to know about me, you'll need to do a spell."

"A spell?" I asked my grandmother.

"Yes, there's a spellbook in this house."

"A spellbook? Really?"

"Is this some kind of sick joke? If yes, you have the worst timing. Your grandmother's funeral is tomorrow!" Scott sat down across from me.

"Sorry Scott, but I'm talking to my grandmother right now," I said and looked at him crossly. "So, where is this special book?" I asked my grandmother point-blank as she looked around the room, seemingly happy about everything that was happening.

"It's in the attic, of course," she said as if I should've known better.

"Of course it is." I rolled my eyes.

"Don't you roll your eyes at me, little girl," my grand-mother said as she followed me up to the attic. Scott followed too, apparently interested in what I was going to do next.

"I know this is all crazy and stuff, but I might actu-ally be able to use this in one of my books," Scott said to himself more than to anyone else. I ignored his comment and went up to the attic.

Of course, as soon as I reached the door and tried to open it, I found it was locked. "Just great, this is just freaking great," I said in frustration.

"Just say these words," my grandmother said as she proceeded to repeat some gibberish.

"Could you say that again?" I said, not really sure what she was talking about.

She repeated the words slowly and told me to

concentrate on the door opening by itself. I did as I was told, and surprisingly enough it worked.

"Is this some kind of magic trick or something?" Scott looked dumbfounded.

I rolled my eyes at him and just ignored his comment. Did he think I was some kind of magician or something? Anyway, the attic itself was dark and dusty and I was looking for a light switch when Rose pointed one out. I noticed that she had a faint glow about her.

"Thanks," I said as I switched the light on.

The attic came to life. It had a lot of stuff in there, a lot of old antiques and stuff like that. But most noticeable of all was a huge trunk in the middle of the vast space.

"Is this it?" I asked my grandmother as I approached the big trunk.

"Good job," Rose said sarcastically.

I ignored her attitude and approached the wooden trunk. Surprisingly enough, the thing was open already. I did not need to say any special word or have a key or anything like that. I looked up at my grandmother in a questioning manner.

"What? The door spell was enough for most people," she said, looking almost defensive about it.

"Sorry, I didn't mean anything by it," I said as I opened the trunk.

What I found inside did not surprise me. A bunch of candles, a bunch of trinkets, talismans, amulets, or whatever they were, I have no idea. But finally, beneath all of that, there was a thick, leather bound, very old-looking book.

I felt the power, the heat, coming off the book almost immediately. My grandmother looked down approvingly as I opened the book. At first, the writing seemed like gibberish or some language that I had never seen before, but then when I looked closer, the letters changed and I could suddenly understand what was written. *Grimoire*, the book said on its first page.

I looked up at my grandmother with a question in my eyes.

"It's a spellbook of sorts," she said as if I should already have known that. "I really should not have let your mother take you away when you were a kid," she said and looked away.

"It's fine, it's fine," I tried to reassure her that she had no choice in the matter. When my mother made up her mind, there was no way of dissuading her from doing what she wanted to do. I knew that better than anyone else, and it took me years to escape her grasp and move out on my own. That was when I moved to New York and met Scott, which was the best decision I had made in my life.

"Come on, girl, get on with it," my grandmother said impatiently.

"This is crazy," Scott said as he looked at me and the

book in my hands. "This looks like gibberish," he said as he took a closer look at what I was reading.

"Scott, just stay calm," I said. "I know what I'm doing," I added even though I had no idea what was going on. In fact, I wasn't even sure I wasn't still dreaming.

I flipped through the book, through the pages, and saw all assortment of spells, formulas, incantations, and all kinds of drawings that I didn't even understand. My grandmother looked down approvingly and told me to keep flipping through the pages until I felt the need to stop. I did as I was told and when I finally reached that page I felt this heat coming off of it especially.

I looked down at the spell I had stopped at and saw that it was a spell that allowed mundanes to peek into the world of the supernatural.

"Come here Scott, and take my hand," I said as I extended my arm to him.

Scott looked at me like I had completely lost it. I couldn't blame him, but we really didn't have time for this. I needed to know if I was crazy or not. If this spell worked, and Scott saw my dead grandmother just as I did, then I would know I wasn't crazy and that she was telling the truth. Otherwise, she could just be a hallucination, and I definitely needed to get some help. Professional help, that is.

"We don't have time for this," I said sternly. Scott

took my hand reluctantly, as I proceeded to say the incantation on the page in front of me.

It was a strange feeling that came over me. The whole room seemed like it was spinning. I wondered if Scott felt the same. Then, something clicked into place.

"Wow," Scott said as he looked around and then focused his eyes on where my dead grandmother was standing.

"You see her too?" I said excitedly.

"Yes, I see an old woman. Scratch that, make that an old see-through woman."

"Fine, fine, talk about me like I'm not even here, fruitcake," my grandmother said.

"You're a feisty one, aren't you?" Scott said as he started to grin from ear to ear.

I wasn't really sure what was happening here, but Scott seemed to be taking this in stride. He had called me crazy for saying the same thing earlier, but now that he was seeing a ghost, he didn't seem to have much trouble with it.

"You seem to be taking this awfully well," I said.

"Well, I can see her now!" Scott said, suddenly excited about the prospect of the spirit world being real.

"We really don't have time for this, kids, let's get back to business," Rose said as she looked from me to Scott then back to me again.

"What business?" Scott asked, now really curious what my dead grandmother actually wanted.

"To solve my murder of course," Rose said, as if it was the most normal thing in the world.

"It's true," I said as I flipped through the pages of the spellbook. I still couldn't believe any of this was real. I expected to wake up at any moment and to feel like a fool. But, I had to admit, that all of this was kind of cool on some level. Magic was real. And not just the wishful thinking, spellcasting, kind of thing that they sold at my grandmother's shop, but real, actual, *supernatural* magic.

"Murdered? You were murdered?" Scott asked my grandmother.

"Of course, why else would I be here?"

"Well, I'm a mystery writer. And a mystery reader, so I think I can definitely help you solve, or figure out, or whatever, who killed you."

"Well, thank you, young man. Now I'm more confident than ever that my murder will go unsolved." My grandmother rolled her dead see-through eyes at Scott.

I couldn't help but laugh. Scott looked at me like he was about to kill me.

"Geez, I was just trying to help." Scott turned away, looking defeated.

"It's okay Scott, that's just the way she is," I said to him, trying to make him feel better. But it was true, my grandmother was kind of weird. She seemed pretty feisty for a dead person.

"Thanks, Rory," Scott said, seemingly feeling a little better about the whole situation.

"We don't have time for this back and forth. Let's just get to the business at hand: my murder."

"Fine," Scott and I said in unison.

"Now that we're all acquainted, why don't we start talking about actually trying to solve my murder, instead of talking about such inconsequential things as who knew what and what knew who," my grandmother started to sound like she was losing her grip on reality.

Both Scott and I looked at her like she was crazy.

"Am I the only one who didn't get any of that?" Scott asked.

"Me neither," I said as I looked at my grandmother like she was crazy not for the first time that night.

"Take that book, and let's go downstairs," Rose said as she started to walk toward the entrance. And then she walked right through the solid wooden door.

I looked at Scott, then I looked at the door she just went through, then I looked at the book in my hands.

"This is going to be interesting," I said as I got up to go.

FOUR

I<small>T</small> <small>WAS STRANGE TO BE FOLLOWING MY GRANDMOTHER'S</small> see-through ghost through the rest of the house. Scott was right on our tail, and I had that big, heavy book in my hands. I could still feel the heat of it in my arms. It was almost too hot to hold.

Rose stopped in the living room and waited for us to catch up. We did pretty soon.

Scott and I sat on the comfortable sofa while my grandmother stood a few feet in front of us, with a disapproving look on her face.

"So, what's next? What are we supposed to do?" I asked her.

"Solve my murder," she said. "What else did you think I wanted you to do?"

"Well, if it was as simple as that, we would already have done it."

"This is kind of cool!" Scott seemed really excited about the idea of solving a murder. I don't know why I was surprised since he read all those books and actually wanted to write them, but this was real life and this was a ghost telling us to solve her murder.

"At least somebody is excited," my grandmother said as she looked down lovingly at Scott. It was the first time she actually looked at him like he was there.

"Thanks," Scott said as he smiled from ear to ear.

I rolled my eyes. In fact, I rolled my eyes so often that it felt like they were going to fall out of my head.

"Rory? What do you say?" Rose asked, suddenly very interested in what I had to say.

"Of course I'll help solve your murder, what kind of granddaughter would I be if I didn't?"

"This is gonna be so much fun," Scott said, all excited about the prospect of solving the murder of a dead witch.

"So does this mean I'm a witch?" I asked my grandmother point-blank.

"Of course, I already told you that."

"Wow, so you guys are actually real-life witches?" Scott said, seemingly really excited about the idea.

"Of course, you silly boy," she said. "Of course we're witches, otherwise, why do you think you're able to see me right now?"

"I guess that makes some kind of sick sense," he said

as he looked from me to my grandmother, to the book in my hands.

Scott reached out for the book and took it into his hands. Surprisingly, the book did not stop him from doing so. But as he flipped through the pages the puzzled look on his face only grew. I knew he could not read the book. Only witches could. Only my grandmother and I could read the words within. I guess that was the way the book protected itself from prying eyes that should not have looked upon it.

"This is gibberish," he said. "Are you actually able to read all this?" Scott asked me point-blank.

"Yeah, it looked like gibberish at first but then I could actually read the whole thing."

"I wish I was able to read this," Scott said, with a sad look in his eyes.

"Don't be silly, boy, you're not a witch so why should you be able to read our book?" Rose said, as if he should've known better.

"There's no need for that," I said to my grandmother. "It's not his fault he's not special like us."

"Thanks, Rory," Scott said, looking like I had actually hurt his feelings.

"I was just joking," I said as I started to giggle. "You must admit, that this is kind of funny."

"There's nothing funny about murder, especially *my* murder," Rose said as she looked at me disapprovingly.

"I gotta say, I agree with your grandmother on this

one," Scott looked away, obviously not amused by my joke.

"You guys are no fun," I said as I took the book back. "This belongs to me."

"Now that that's out of the way, can we get back to the task at hand? Mainly, solving my murder."

"Fine, fine, but first I need to learn about all this witch stuff. If another witch murdered you, I need to learn as much as I can, don't I?"

"Yes, I suppose that's true."

"Another witch? Why would another witch murder you?" Scott asked as he looked from me to my grandmother.

"If I knew that, my dear boy, I wouldn't need you two, would I?" My grandmother seemed annoyed by the both of us.

It was strange. It was surreal. I couldn't believe any of this was actually happening. Here I was, talking to the ghost of my dead grandmother, and she was asking me to solve her murder. "Where should we start?" I asked in desperation.

"My funeral is a good place as any," my grandmother said. "I'm pretty sure the murderer will be there to gloat."

"I do have one question, though," I said. "Why did you leave all of this to me? Why not to my cousin?"

"Your cousin Rhi already has magic. You, on the other hand, needed to be lured back into the fold.

Don't worry about Rhi, I left her all my money. You get my house and shop, she gets the rest. It's more than fair."

"I didn't think of it like that," I said.

THE NEXT MORNING I woke up groggy and confused. I wasn't sure that what happened yesterday really happened, but when I looked over in the corner of my room I saw my grandmother standing there. It definitely wasn't a dream.

Before I had a chance to comment I heard the doorbell. That must've been what woke me up in the first place.

"Who could it be?" I kept asking myself as I made my way down the stairs.

Once I reached the door and looked through the peephole I saw a familiar face. I knew she was going to show up and was hoping she would not.

It was my mother. That's all that needed to be said.

I opened the door reluctantly and when my mother saw my haircut she immediately rolled her eyes.

"You really need to do something about that hair, Rory." My mother said as she made her way past me. Just as I was about to close the door, a large group of caterers followed suit.

"What is all this?" I asked my mother as I followed her into the living room.

"For after the funeral," she said. "In polite society, people gather after the funeral."

I had no response to that, at least not any response my mother would like to hear.

I looked up the stairs and saw Scott standing there. He looked scared to go down, and I rolled my eyes at him. I couldn't blame him, though, because my mother *was* insufferable.

"The lawyer should be here in a couple of hours," my mother said as she dialed a number into her phone.

I asked her if my sister was coming.

"She and Brandon are on their way. They should be here within the hour."

Sam was my perfect sister. At least according to what my mother always said. And Brandon, a lawyer, was my sister's fiancé.

Once my mother started yelling at her phone, demanding to talk to a manager, something about the caterers getting something wrong, I quickly made my way upstairs to make myself presentable.

I ran into Scott.

"I've managed to slip her demonic gaze!" He said as he followed me back upstairs.

I rolled my eyes. "Scott, I'm pretty sure she won't bite."

"You don't sound so sure about that yourself!" I heard Scott's voice say as I opened the door to my room.

Then I checked my grandmother's room. Even the cat wasn't there.

Surprisingly, Rose was nowhere to be found. I wondered where she went to. Either way, I needed to get ready for the funeral, and then for the lawyer, and then apparently for the gathering *after* the funeral.

While I wasn't overjoyed to see my mother, I had to admit that she did take care of things, so that made it a lot easier for the rest of us.

I wondered if she knew her mother left everything to me.

The rest of the day went by in a flurry. It took several hours for everything to be set up to my mother's specifications.

We made our way to the church, Scott by my side.

"Have you seen my grandmother?" I asked Scott as we made our way inside the church.

"No, why are you asking?"

"After my mother arrived, she disappeared."

"Wouldn't you if she was your daughter?"

"I guess you have a point there," I said.

We sat in the front row with my mother waiting for my sister to arrive. My mother grew restless, but when she saw Sam coming in with her very handsome fiancé, her face lit up.

Of course, I'd never seen that kind of look directed at me. I was a constant disappointment to my mother, as she would often say right to my face. For example, when she saw what I was wearing, she had to comment on how horrible she thought it was.

The priest came to the podium and said some quick words about the ceremony being taken over by someone else, and he didn't seem happy about it. Neither was my mother. Apparently, she wasn't aware the priest wasn't going to lead this ceremony.

I myself was not surprised. Wasn't my grandmother a witch?

"Thank you for gathering here today, to celebrate the life of Rose Wiltz," an older woman in a white robe said.

The rest of the ceremony was quite dull. I tried to look around to spot any potential suspects, but no one really jumped out at me.

A collective sigh of relief could be felt once the ceremony was done. I had a quick word with the woman who officiated the funeral, but she said she was called in by Rhi and that she hadn't talked to Rose in years.

I didn't have a chance to interrogate any of the other attendees because my mother pulled me back and gave me a stern look.

"Stay away from those people," she hissed.

FIVE

AFTER THE FUNERAL IT WAS TIME TO GO BACK TO THE house and get the legal part taken care of.

"This is Brandon," Sam said as she introduced her fiancé.

Brandon was handsome and tall with short blond hair and had the kind of smile that could probably win over any woman (even some men) within a ten-mile radius. I, on the other hand, wasn't impressed. I shook his hand and smiled, but inside I was thinking that he seemed too good to be true. Handsome? Check. Great job? Check. Nice and polite? Double check.

I pulled Sam aside and asked her where she met him.

"He worked on a case for my boss," she said as she smiled from ear to ear. Sam had long blonde hair, the exact kind of hair my mother approved of. Not the dyed black hair I was sporting. I noticed that she couldn't take her eyes off of Brandon.

"That's nice," I said. "Did you do a background check?"

Sam laughed. "Rory, don't be ridiculous. Maybe if you trusted people more you wouldn't be single right now."

I sighed. "We're not talking about me, we're talking about you."

"Come on girls," our mother called to us from the living room. It seemed that we were the only people holding up the whole proceedings.

Scott was in a corner by himself so I joined him. My mother sent me a death glare which told me that I needed to sit with the family on the couch.

"Sorry Scott, gotta go," I said.

"It's fine," he reassured me, as he took another bite of the pie on his plate.

I sat next to Sam, who sat next to my mother. Our cousin Rhi sat next to me.

The lawyer was looking through the will as he sat across from us on a comfy sofa.

He looked up and adjusted his glasses. Once he started talking I realized I had already talked to him on the phone.

"My granddaughter Rory Wiltz is the sole beneficiary of my house and my business, my shop Book & Candle." I instinctively looked around but didn't spot my grandmother's ghost. I wondered why she didn't make an appearance.

My mother's reaction was clear. She did not like what she was hearing one bit.

My sister seemed happy for me.

"To my granddaughter Rhiannon Wiltz, I leave all my savings. To my granddaughter, Samantha Wiltz, I leave my rare book collection. To my daughter, Morgan Wiltz, I leave absolutely nothing."

"Vindictive old hag," my mother said under her breath and I heard a few gasps around the room. My mother took hold of her drink and gulped half of it in one go.

And that was that. Sam didn't seem too upset that she only got some old books. I hoped they were worth something.

"I didn't expect to get anything!" She said as she joined Brandon. It was just like Sam to take the whole thing in stride. She probably figured that my grandmother thought I needed it more. After all, I was a struggling waitress in New York while Sam lived in New York City and had a successful career with one of the biggest companies in the world. She didn't need grandmother's help. I on the other hand did.

My mother was in search of another drink and her carefully crafted facade seemed to be cracking.

"Well, mother is not taking it so well," I told Sam when Brandon went to get a drink of his own. Maybe he was a closet alcoholic? What? There had to be something wrong with that guy.

"She'll get over it. On the way here all she could talk about was how she wasn't expecting anything at all."

"Sounds just like her," I said.

"Sounds just like who?" My mother startled me when she snuck up behind us.

"Oh, I was just talking about grandma leaving me basically everything," I recovered quickly, I just hoped my mother bought it.

My mother took another gulp from her drink, which she seemed to have already refilled. "You can't keep any of it, you know that?"

"Why can't I?" I asked. It was mine to keep after all.

"Your grandmother...my mother...well, let's just say she was more than eccentric. She believed some strange things. No daughter of mine will be involved in any of that. You'll sell this old house, and you'll definitely get rid of that witch shop of hers."

"You say all of that like you have any say in the matter. Grandma left those things to me, not you, so I think it's my choice what I do with it."

I could see by the look on my mother's face that she was at her limits with me.

"Do what you want. But if you come crying to me for help, you'll know what the answer will be."

With that, my mother left me and my sister to ourselves. Brandon also made his appearance and resumed his position by Sam's side. Even though I was a total cynic when it came to all that lovey dovey stuff, I had to admit that they did make a very good-looking couple.

"Well, before she burns the whole house down, we should probably be on our way back," Sam said as she took a sip of her own drink, which was a nonalcoholic ice tea.

"So soon? You just got here!"

"Sadly, NYC waits for nobody," Sam said. "Brandon and I only managed to get two days off, and even that took some convincing."

"Maybe living in a small town like Hazelville isn't such a bad thing," I said.

Sam laughed. "I never thought I'd hear you say those words."

"Could you excuse us for a minute," I said to Brandon. I needed to ask my sister some questions that definitely needed some privacy. I pulled her out back on the patio. I watched as Brandon approached Scott for some conversation. Scott seemed flustered at first (Brandon was gorgeous after all) but recovered fairly quickly.

I turned back to my sister. "Are you pregnant?"

"What?" Sam looked shocked. "What makes you say that?"

"Your drink. You were never one to pass up an alcoholic beverage."

Sam groaned. "I can't keep anything from you, can I?"

"Why wouldn't you tell me?" I had to admit that I was a little disappointed that she hadn't confided in me. Sure, we didn't see much of each other in the past few years, but I still thought we were close.

"It's early. We were going to tell everyone once it was for certain."

"Oh," I said, suddenly feeling like an asshole. I don't know why I was making such a big deal out of it, anyway: wasn't I the one keeping a pretty huge secret from her?

"Do you remember grandmother?" I asked her. Sam was two years older than me, so I hoped she had more memories than me.

"Honestly, not really. I remember that mother never let us see her that much. And then when we moved after dad left, we didn't get to see her at all. Why?"

"Just wondering. I still can't believe she left me all of this." I looked up at the huge house. Not in a million years would I have seen myself living in a small town in a house such as this. If I hadn't seen my grandmother's ghost and found out that I was a witch, I wasn't so sure I wouldn't have done what my mother suggested.

"It's pretty great, isn't it? I guess she knew that you needed it the most."

"Hey! There's no need for that. I was doing quite well for myself."

Sam smiled. She knew I was full of it but decided not to call me out on it.

"Do you remember anything strange about our grandmother?"

"Besides the whole witch thing?" Sam asked. "Not really. I always thought of her as a New Age hippy."

"Hmm, I guess she was in some ways. Have you ever experienced anything...strange?"

"What do you mean?"

"I mean...like a dream, a vision, a premonition...I don't know."

"Rory, are you alright?" My sister put a hand on my shoulder, looking worried about me.

"Yeah, yeah, It's just that I've been having some strange dreams lately."

"Can't say I have," Sam said. "It's probably this house. It is pretty creepy. At least you have Scott so you're not alone here."

I looked back into the house. Scott, Rhi, and Brandon seemed to be enjoying a lively conversation.

"Are you just marrying him because you're pregnant?"

"I'm marrying him because I love him," Sam said and I could see in her eyes that she did love him. I just hoped he loved her as well.

"What about you?" Sam asked. "When will you find somebody to love?"

I laughed. "Don't be cheesy, Sam. You know I don't believe in any of that crap."

It was true: I was not a romantic at heart, though I did have a few relationships here and there. When the guys tried to get serious, I bolted. I'd never gone to therapy, but if I had to guess, I'd say that it was probably my absent father and my overbearing mother that were at fault.

"Sam, get ready. Our cab will be here soon," my mother poked her head through the screen door. "Rory," she said as she looked at me with that look of disapproval. "I hope you think about what I've said to you."

"The thing about my hair or the one about my clothes?" I asked, not able to resist.

"You know what about," my mother said as she rolled her eyes. What can I say? It was a family trait. "Though it wouldn't hurt to go back to your natural color and find something besides black to wear."

With that, my mother gave me an awkward hug that lasted a lot longer than I was comfortable with. I hugged Sam tight and told her to call me anytime she needed.

The car was already outside waiting for them once we went back inside. Brandon gave me a quick hug as well.

"If you hurt my sister..." I said and left the rest to his imagination when Sam and my mother were out of earshot.

Brandon grinned wide. "You don't have to worry about that," he reassured me and joined them.

I stood by the door and waved them off. Little by little, the rest of the crowd left as well, all offering condolences for my loss and some leaving more food that would never be eaten.

In the end, it was only Scott, Rhi and me in the house.

"Finally," I heard my grandmother's voice behind me and nearly jumped out of my skin. "They're all gone."

Rhi looked at our grandmother and smiled. "Nice to see you again, grandma," she said.

SIX

"You can see her?" I asked Rhi, though I already knew the answer.

"Of course," Rhi said. "I'm a witch, just like you."

"Well, I don't know about that. I had to do a spell so that I could see her, but you can just see her naturally?"

"Once you've been practicing magic for a while, you start to see the world a bit differently," Rhi said and shrugged her shoulders.

I looked over at my see-through grandmother. "A lot differently," I said.

Rhi laughed. "I guess so. So are you all caught up on this witch business?"

"I know the basics," I said, taking a look at my grandmother. "Why weren't you here earlier?" I asked her, genuinely curious why she wasn't there to see if her killer had made an appearance.

"Think about it," Rose said. "A witch murdered me. Most witches can see or sense ghosts. Do you really think that would have been a good idea?"

"I guess I see your point there," I said.

"This is great!" Rhi said as she looked from me to our grandmother to Scott, who was sitting on the couch with a mystery in his hands.

"What's so great?" I really had no idea what she was talking about.

"We can work together to solve granny's murder!"

"I told you it was cool," Scott said as he looked up from his paperback.

"You two are crazy. We don't even have a clue. And it's not like there was anybody at the funeral that looked suspicious. Did you notice anyone, Rhi? You've been a witch far longer than I."

"No," Rhi said. "I don't think so."

"You probably weren't even paying attention," Rose chided us. "At this rate, my murder will never be solved."

Her words piqued Scott's interest and he left his book on the couch and joined us.

"I said we were going to help you, and we will. Right, guys?" He looked from me to Rhi. Neither of us seemed too certain about that fact.

"It's hard," Rhi admitted. "I tried making a list of suspects today and I couldn't even come up with one."

All three of us looked at Rose.

"I told you I don't remember..." She suddenly sounded a lot more defensive than was necessary.

"We know that," Scott said. "But you must have an idea. Any enemies? People that you think might wish you harm?"

Rose floated back and forth across the room. It was kind of unnerving but at the same time cool. I guess if I was a ghost I wouldn't bother walking either.

Suddenly she stopped in mid stride and floated on over to where the three of us were standing.

"The Crowleys!" She announced, as if that name meant anything to me.

"Hmm, that name sounds familiar," Rhi said.

"It should," Rose said. "They used to live in the house across the street. They had two sons. You and Rory played with them if I remember correctly."

"What were their names? The sons I mean?" I asked, faint memories of playing with some boys when I was younger. I wasn't sure if the memories were real or if my mind created false ones just because of the suggestion.

Rose seemed deep in thought. "Carver and...Hunter, I want to say. But it wasn't the sons I had a problem with, it was their parents."

"How so?" Scott asked, suddenly looking very interested in what Rose had to say. I wondered if he was plotting a mystery novel as we spoke.

"Well, their father and mother, Margaret and Charles if I'm not mistaken, had opened an occult shop at the same time I did mine. Needless to say, my business flourished while theirs didn't. Eventually, they had to move and start over I suppose. But before they did, Margaret came over one day and accused me of cheating. Casting spells to ruin their business and other such nonsense."

I looked at grandma Rose suspiciously. "Are you sure you didn't do anything of the sort?"

"Of course not," she looked offended and I immediately regretted even asking the question. After all, the woman left all her property to me. "I had the better location and the better product. It was as mundane as that," she said.

"Can you think of anyone else, Mrs. Wiltz?" Scott asked.

"Call me Rose," she said with a stern look on her face. "There was never a Mr. Wiltz to speak of. Wiltz is a maiden name passed down through the generations in my family."

"I noticed that earlier," Scott said. "Every generation has the same last name. How is that? Don't any Wiltz women ever get married?"

"Oh, you bet we do." Rose winked. "I myself have been married three times. But since the men in our family don't tend to stick around, either because of death or their own stupidity, we never take their names."

"That's...interesting," Scott said. I could see that he was trying to work out the logistics of it in his head.

Honestly, I wasn't sure myself how it worked out. If there ever was a woman to take on another name in our family, it would have been my mother.

"But enough about that," Rose said. "The only thing we should be focusing on now is my murder."

"Yeah, about that," Scott said. "Why did the police rule it an accident?"

"Because they're idiots," offered Rhi.

"Exactly," Rose agreed. "An old woman falls down the stairs: it must be an accident!"

"Well, I can't say I really blame them," I said carefully. "How are you so sure it was murder if you don't even remember anything?"

"I already told you. If it was just an accident, I would remember and I would have already moved on to the next world."

"There's an afterlife?" Scott asked, seeming very interested in the subject. For as long as I'd known him, he seemed pretty agnostic bordering on atheist on all subjects spiritual. But I guess talking to a ghost of a witch could change anybody's mind on the matter.

"Yes," Rose said carefully. "But that's all I can say on the matter."

"Figures," Scott said, looking pretty defeated.

"As fun as this is, I have to get back to the store," Rhi said as she made her way to the door. It seemed strange to me that all of this was so normal to her, but then again she was a witch so I guess it made sense.

"I'll come with you," I said as I went to get my purse.

"That's right," Rhi said. "You're my boss now, aren't you?" There wasn't much judgment in her tone, but I still felt uncomfortable with the whole situation.

"I'm coming, too," Scott said quickly as he picked up the paperback he was reading. He looked over at Rose's ghostly form. "Sorry, it would just be weird to be here alone with you."

"I understand," Rose said, looking like she was disappointed. "But there's no reason I can't go with you lot."

I looked over at Rhiannon. "Is this true?"

Rhi nodded. "Yeah, why wouldn't she be able to come with us?"

"I just thought that she was stuck here, in this house," I said.

"I died in the shop. If I was to be stuck anywhere it would be there," Rose said and I felt like an idiot.

"Of course," I said. "So how does this work? Do you drive with us or can you teleport there or something?"

"Sadly, I cannot do that yet. I haven't been a ghost long enough. I can certainly fly to there, but it would probably be faster to go with you lot."

So that was how all four of us piled into the car. Scott and Rose were in the back while I was in the front. Rhi was driving.

It took around five minutes to get to the shop. I

shouldn't have been surprised. Hazelville was a pretty small town.

Rhi closed the door behind us as she flipped the sign from closed to open.

"So, what's up?" Rhi asked me when she took her place behind the counter. "Did you have anything in mind?"

"This is the scene of the crime, isn't it?" I simply said.

SEVEN

Rose flew from one end of the store to another, and then she flew to the back. We all followed her.

We found her at the bottom of the stairs where her body had been found.

"I knew it was going to end one day, I just didn't know it was going to end like this," she said, obviously bummed by the whole affair.

I reached out and put a comforting hand on her shoulder but my hand went right through her. "Oh," I said.

Rose looked back with a sad expression on her face. "If only I could remember what happened."

"Maybe being here will help," Scott offered. "At least that's what I've read. But of course, all studies regarding that involved people who had actual brains."

"What did you just say to me, young man?" Rose

looked pissed. She flew toward Scott and he fumbled backward, almost falling on his ass.

"It *was* pretty rude," I agreed with Rose as I walked over to where they were. I might have agreed with my grandmother, but I didn't want her to scare my best friend to death.

"I didn't mean it like that!" Scott quickly said. "I meant you don't have a physical body! Of course you have a brain...or do you? I'm not actually sure how that works..."

"Brainpower is overrated," Rose said sternly. "Us witches know that it's all about the mind, and as you can see, the mind can exist independent of the brain."

"Yes! That makes sense," Scott quickly said. Rose backed off and so did I.

I looked back to where they had found the body. Then I looked at the stairs leading up.

"What's up there?" I asked Rose.

"Presumably something worth killing for," she said.

"Where's the key?"

"That I do not know," she said. "I'm pretty sure I left it to you in my will."

"Hmm, the lawyer didn't say anything about it. Maybe it came with one of the sets of keys I got." I rummaged through my purse and took out the two sets of keys. One for the shop and then another for the house.

Rose looked over my shoulder as I flipped through

each set. "Any of these look right?" I asked as I lifted each up to the light.

"This one!" Rose said when she spotted the right key. It was with the set belonging to the shop, which only made sense.

Just as I started to walk up the stairs, a deafening sound broke through the anticipatory silence.

We all jumped up in fright, even Rose.

"What the hell was that?" Scott asked as he tried to compose himself.

"I guess we'll have to go and see," I said, but made no move. "You're the closest to the door," I told Scott. "And you're a man, so..."

"That's totally sexist! Just because I'm a man doesn't mean I deserve to die! What if it's Rose's killer?"

"I'm not going out there alone," Rhi said. "I think we should go as a group."

"Oh for heaven's sake, I'm already dead, I'll check it out," Rose said as she flew past us and disappeared around the corner.

"It's fine!" We heard her yell back a couple of agonizing seconds later.

This time, Scott didn't mind leading the way to the front of the shop.

The source of the noise was clear as day now. The front window was shattered and a large rock lay a few feet away.

I reached down and picked it up, careful not to touch

the broken glass, then I quickly returned to the register where the rest of them were standing. I didn't want to be in the way if someone decided to throw another rock.

I unwrapped the paper.

"*Close the shop or else!*" The note said in red marker. Or was it something more sinister?

I lifted the note to my nose and smelled the familiar and unpleasant alcoholic scent. "Definitely a marker," I said more to myself than anyone else.

"Can't you see who did this?" I asked my grandmother.

"Probably some local children. How rude, isn't it?" She said without moving an inch.

"I meant can't you go fly after them?"

"They're long gone by now," she said. "Would you stick around if you did something such as this?"

"I guess not," I admitted reluctantly.

Before I had a chance to say anything else, I heard sirens in the distance.

"Crap!" Scott said. "I was really looking forward to what was up in that room."

"Me too!" Rhi agreed, and I started to wonder why I was surrounded by such juveniles.

"Then at least one good thing came out of this... mess," Rose said as she looked at all the broken glass. "Only Rory has the permission to enter that room. I left it to her."

Rhi didn't look happy by the announcement but she didn't say anything. Scott rolled his eyes.

"First, she's a witch, now she gets a special room. Life's not fair!" He complained.

"That's the smartest thing I've heard you say, kid," Rose said as she looked out the broken window. "The police will be here in less than a minute," she announced.

I looked out the window and realized that she was right. "Crap. How are we going to explain all this?"

"Explain?" Rhi asked, incredulous. "Someone just vandalized *us*, not the other way around."

I almost forgot that Book & Candle belonged to me. Then it dawned on me that I was going to have to pay for repairs with money I did not have.

"Maybe I'm selling this place after all," I said to the shock of everyone in the room.

"Well, I'm not buying if that's what you were thinking," said a stranger as he entered the shop.

I was taken aback by how handsome he was but managed to get my head out of the gutters pretty quickly.

"And who the hell are you?"

He moved his leather jacket out of the way to show a badge and a gun that were hidden there.

"I'm Detective Morgan and I've come here to see what the problem is."

EIGHT

"PROBLEM? WHAT PROBLEM? DID SOMEBODY CALL THE cops on us?"

Strangely enough, it wasn't me who uttered those words, but Scott.

The detective made a point of looking around the shop and all the shattered glass.

"Oh," Scott uttered as he scuttled away behind a bookshelf.

"May I?" The detective asked as he reached out to take the rock from my hand. It was quite heavy so I didn't mind giving it to him at all.

"Quite the welcoming message, isn't it?" he said as he looked up and smiled. The combination of his blue eyes and short dark hair, paired with that slightly mischievous and playful smile, was almost too much for me. Was this cop flirting with me or was this how he talked to everyone? I didn't know which would have been worse.

"No, it isn't," I agreed.

"You're Rory Wiltz, am I right?" he asked and I nodded in response. "Welcome to Hazelville, I guess."

"Thanks," I said sarcastically. "And what's a detective going to do about this mess? A regular copper just wasn't available or...?"

"We're understaffed if you must know and I'm a transfer from Chicago."

"What did you do to deserve that?" I joked, but Detective Morgan looked away uncomfortably. He recovered pretty quick, though.

"Do any of you have any idea who could have done this?" he asked, sounding like he was losing his patience.

Then I saw the strangest sight: a hand manifesting itself through the detective's chest. I almost screamed out in horror before I realized what it was.

"What is it, Miss?" He asked as he looked down at his chest, which looked quite welcoming by the way. "You look like you've seen a ghost."

"It was worth a shot," my grandmother said as she flew back to her original position. She still observed the detective with a strange expression on her ghostly face.

"Maybe I *have* seen a ghost," I said and immediately regretted the words.

The detective looked around the shop. At the candles, the herbs, the books, the spell kits.

"Ha ha," he said. "Very funny. But this here is a serious matter, so if any of you have any ideas I'd like to know about it. The sooner you do the sooner I'll be out of your hair."

"If we knew, we wouldn't be standing here dumbfounded, would we Detective Morgan?" Rhi said as she crossed her arms and looked at the detective like he had done something horrible to her. "How about instead of focusing on petty pranks, you reopen my grandmother's case?"

"It was an accident. Open and shut. You already know that Ms. Wiltz."

Rhi turned away, the look of disgust clear on her face.

"How are you so sure it was an accident?" I asked the detective as I drew him aside from the mess.

He sighed. "I've seen plenty of murders in my time, and this simply wasn't one of them. The coroner agreed with me," he added as he looked over in Rhi's direction.

"I bet if she wasn't the owner of this shop and a rumored witch, it wouldn't so black and white now would it?"

It was clear that Rhi was no fan of Detective Morgan.

"I'll have to report this," he said as he handed me a card. "If you think of anything, don't hesitate to call. By the way," he added before he was out the door. "Are you planning on staying in town or not?"

"I was planning on staying, at least for a little while, but after all this, I'm not so sure." It was true, the whole vandalism thing made me reluctant to make Hazelville my permanent home.

"Well, don't let the locals scare you off. I doubt any of them are capable of doing any serious damage."

"Tell that to my grandmother," Rhi called out as the detective went back to his car.

"Was that really necessary?" I asked Rhi after the detective drove off. He didn't drive a police vehicle, and I wasn't surprised at all. There was nothing regular about the guy.

"Who's side are you on, cousin?" Rhi asked me, suddenly all her anger transferring from the detective to me.

I did not like it one bit. Just before I said something I might regret later, Rose swooped in between us.

"Girls, there's no need to fight. This should only make you want to work that much harder to solve my murder. Show that copper just how dumb he is. Handsome, yes, but dumb."

I couldn't argue with that. "I'm sorry if I came off as not caring."

"I'm sorry I snapped at you. Do I still have a job?" Rhi asked jokingly, though I could see real worry behind her smile.

"Of course. This place is as much yours as it is mine, no matter what the will has to say about it."

Rose was standing and smiling there one second, and the next she was gone. I had not even seen her move.

"Well look what the cat dragged into town," I heard a man's voice say behind me.

I turned around and saw a tall guy with shoulder length brown hair and piercing green eyes.

"Rory Wiltz," he said as if he knew me. "Aren't you going to say hello to your old pal Hunter?"

NINE

"HUNTER?" I SAID, NOT BELIEVING WHAT I WAS SEEING. "Hunter Crowley?"

"Oh crap," I heard Scott say behind me.

Hunter looked down at the mess and carefully entered the shop in his leather boots.

"What's that supposed to mean?" He asked Scott.

"Nothing," Scott said nervously. "I was just commenting on all this mess."

"I'm sure you were," Hunter said. Then he turned his gaze on Rhi. "Little Rhiannon all grown up. Is that really you?"

Rhi backed away a little.

"He's powerful, Rory. Be careful."

Hunter smiled a devilish smile as he looked all around and then back at me. "I come here in peace, girls...and guy," he added when he saw Scott giving him a death stare.

"Why do you come at all?" I asked point-blank. "We just buried our grandmother today and somebody just vandalized her shop. We're a little busy at the moment."

"That's why I'm here," he said as he looked at me straight in the eyes. I could feel his immense power now. I knew exactly what Rhi was warning me about.

"What do you mean?"

"It was a strange coincidence I guess, or call it fate if you will. I just arrived in town and I was on my way here when I spotted a couple of hooligans making their escape in their beat up pick-up truck."

"Why didn't you go after them?" I asked.

"Do I look like a cop?" He definitely didn't. "I didn't think so. I did something better, though," he said as he took out a piece of paper from his jacket pocket. "I wrote down their license plate number."

"Great!" I said. "Let's go to the police station and report them."

"Exactly what I was thinking," Hunter said and smiled. "My motorcycle is at the back of the building."

Rhi drew me away from him. "Are you sure you want to do this?" She asked me.

"Yeah, you don't even know this dude," Scott whispered.

I looked back in Hunter's direction. He just smiled that smile and nodded.

"It's Hunter, from across the street, remember?" I looked around but there was no sign of Rose. I guess she sensed another witch nearby and high-tailed it out of there. I wondered if she knew exactly what witch it was.

"Remember what grandma said..." Rhi whispered as she gave Hunter the stink eye.

"Exactly," I said. "That guy over there, he's our prime suspect and he practically offered himself up on a silver platter. How could I refuse an opportunity like that?"

"You have a point," Scott agreed. "Just be careful and call or text if anything weird happens, okay?"

I nodded. "You know I can take care of myself."

I PUT on the helmet he offered and hopped on behind Hunter. A rush of adrenaline went through me as I heard the loud roar of the engine.

"You ever ridden on one of these?" Hunter asked as he put his own helmet on.

"Yeah, but it's been awhile," I said, and to my surprise I found myself telling him the truth.

It didn't take long for us to arrive at the police station. I saw that Detective Morgan's car was already parked right out front.

"Good," I said.

"What's good?"

"The detective who responded to our little

vandalism incident is here. You can give him the license plate number yourself."

Hunter nodded in agreement. "I heard about your grandmother. Sorry for your loss."

"Are you really?" I said as I handed him the helmet.

"Of course, why would you think I wasn't?"

"Nothing, it's just that I remember hearing about the rivalry between her and your parents."

Hunter laughed. "That's ancient history," he reassured me, but I wasn't so sure I was convinced by his blasé demeanor.

We went inside the building. It was only then that I realized how idiotic it was that I was going to the police with a guy who might be involved with my grandmother's death.

The receptionist at the front desk was an older lady with white curly hair and a bad attitude if her phone answering skills were any indication.

"Sir, that's not a matter for the police, but if you continue wasting my time by calling here, it certainly will be," then the receptionist hung up.

"What do you lot want?" She looked from me to Hunter. Hunter smiled his best smile while I still tried to think of what to say.

"We're here to report a crime," Hunter said without missing a beat. I looked at the receptionist's name tag and saw her name was Betty. "May we speak to Detective..."

"Morgan," I quickly offered. "Detective Morgan. He was at my shop earlier. Someone threw a rock through our window."

"Yeah, yeah, I don't need your whole life story sweetheart. His office is that way," she pointed behind her at the back of the small police station. "You can't miss it."

"Thanks," I said instinctively, though I made sure to put a sarcastic tone in there for her benefit.

The door to the office was open and I saw that it said Det. Jack Morgan.

Before either I or Hunter had a chance to knock, the detective looked up from some paperwork he was reading. When he saw me, he immediately covered what he was looking at with some manila envelopes. What was that about?

"How may I help you, Ms. Wiltz?" He asked with a smile on his face. Then he saw Hunter standing behind me. "And you are?"

"I'm Hunter Crowley," Hunter said as he moved past me and extended his hand. The detective took it reluctantly.

"Quite the grip you got there," the detective said as he took back his hand and proceeded to massage it.

Hunter smiled. "Thank you. I'm here to report a crime. I saw the people who vandalized Book & Candle."

Jack Morgan looked surprised. "That's quite fortuitous. I didn't think we'd get any tips so soon."

Hunter handed him the paper with the license plate number. "Hope that helps. I saw them drive off after committing the deed. Didn't really get a good look at them, though. I've only come back to town today."

"Oh? You used to live here?"

"Many years ago. Now I'm thinking of coming back," Hunter said as he looked back at me and smiled. "I certainly hope that what happened today isn't any indication of the new attitude around here."

"No, no," Jack said. "Well, I've only been here for a couple of months, but it seems like a pretty quiet town so far."

The detective took the piece of paper and entered the number into his computer.

"Ah, yes, that makes sense," he said as he looked at his screen, which was out of my field of vision of course.

I moved past Hunter and tried to see who it was for myself, but the detective quickly closed the screen.

"Why'd you do that? They vandalized my shop. I have a right to know who they are."

"They're a couple of local teens. Petty criminals at best," the detective offered.

"I don't care if they're in kindergarten," I said. "They're paying for that broken window one way or another."

"Of course, but let me handle this. It's my job after all," he said, looking more than a bit annoyed.

"You wish you were back in Chicago working on high-profile cases, don't you?" I asked him.

Detective Morgan shook his head. "Don't worry, Ms. Wiltz, I will take care of this for you and I will inform you when I have more information."

"She has a right to know who vandalized her shop. What if they decided to come back and do something worse?" Hunter spoke up, and I was glad he did. It seemed like the detective wasn't taking my case seriously at all.

The two men exchanged long looks. It looked like neither was willing to back down.

I stepped between the two of them because I really didn't have time for this.

"Boys, behave," I said and they both groaned in annoyance at my interruption.

Hunter was the first to step back, though he didn't look happy about it.

"Let's go," I said and Hunter nodded.

"If something happens to Rory, it's on you detective," he said before we high-tailed it out of there.

I felt kind of sorry for Detective Morgan. He looked pretty bored and miserable, but it was his job after all and it needed to be done. If he didn't want to do it, he should have moved to a bigger town with more crime.

"You didn't have to say all those things," I said as we walked out of the police station. "I could have told him myself."

"Were you going to?"

"Of course," I said, though I wasn't really sure if I would have.

"Where to next?" Hunter asked as he offered me the helmet.

"Back to the shop, of course," I said without missing a beat.

"How about we go for drinks and catch up on old times instead?" Hunter smiled that devilish smile again and I found that I couldn't say no to him.

After all, if my grandmother was right, he might have been involved in her murder.

"Fine," I said. "Though I can't promise much. All I remember is some vague stuff when we were kids."

"Don't worry, Rory, I'll jog your memory."

TEN

"Wow, I can't believe we did that!" I said and laughed as I took another sip of my rum and coke. What can I say, I'm pretty boring when it comes to my drink choices.

Hunter himself was drinking scotch on the rocks.

"Do you remember the look on her face when you got back home with all that mud on you?" Hunter asked.

"Oh God, I can't believe I'd forgotten that. But now that we've caught up on our past, I think it's time you tell me what happened after you left Hazelville."

Suddenly Hunter looked uncomfortable. He looked away and breathed in deeply, but when his gaze turned back on me, he was his old fun-loving self.

"My parents decided we needed a new start far away from here. I hear the same thing happened to you?"

"Yeah," I said. "My mother moved us before I started

high school. She said that there was nothing here for us."

"And here you are now. With a new house and a business to run."

"I'm not so sure if I'm sticking around, though. Especially after what happened today."

"That *was* strange. You would think your grandmother would have some wards to prevent that kind of thing."

"Wards?"

"It's like a magical protective barrier that should have prevented what happened today. I can't believe you don't know that."

"My mother wasn't a huge fan of my grandmother, so when we moved I barely had any contact with her. I've only found out about this witch stuff yesterday. It's all new to me and I have so much to learn." As soon as that last sentence came out of my mouth I knew what it sounded like.

"I'm more than willing to teach you a few tricks, if you want," Hunter offered.

"I have my cousin Rhiannon. I'll be fine. But what I'm really interested in is why are you back in town all of a sudden?"

"Maybe I was feeling nostalgic," Hunter offered but he knew I wasn't buying it. "Fine, I heard about your grandmother and had to see it for myself. I didn't make the funeral so I decided to stop by the shop."

I didn't know what to say to that. "Ding dong the witch is dead kind of deal?"

Hunter laughed. "Something like that."

I didn't find that remotely funny.

"No, really, what's the reason you're back?"

Hunter looked away.

"It's a personal matter. A family matter."

"I know how that goes," I admitted. "Though the cause of my family's troubles is pretty clear. My mother and her incessant need for control."

"That's why you moved to New York, wasn't it? How was that?"

"If it was a success I wouldn't be here talking to you, would I?" I said as I took a sip of my drink. This time, I needed it. My mother. My failure in New York. It was all something I didn't need to think about right now.

"Don't sweat it," Hunter said as he put a hand on my shoulder. I knew he was doing it to comfort me, but I still flinched away. But not before I noticed the warmth of his touch. It reminded me of the grimoire and its magical heat. "Sorry if I did something wrong."

"No, it's not that. There was just something about your touch. Something strange that reminded me of something even stranger."

Hunter laughed. "That doesn't sound good."

I laughed, too. "I guess it doesn't." I made a show of looking at the time on my cell phone. "I should really get back to the shop. I don't want to leave Rhi alone there."

"Isn't your friend with her? What was his name, Scott was it?"

If I knew Scott, he was probably in that bookshop across the way.

"Yeah, I guess. Still, it's my shop and the repair people are coming. I should probably be overseeing it."

"If you say so."

Hunter seemed distant all of a sudden. "I might stop by one of these days," he said.

"Stocking up on witch supplies?"

"Something like that."

It was a nice enough day so I decided to walk back to the shop. It would only take five minutes to walk.

I wondered what the deal was with Hunter. I knew there was something more to his story than he was sharing. But now that I caught up with him and actually remembered some of the times we spent together as kids, it was hard for me to believe that he was a murderer.

When I entered the store, the glass was already cleaned up and the repair people were already installing the new window.

"That was fast," I said to Rhi when I joined her by the register.

"Yeah, I guess it's a slow day for them. Thank goodness we got vandalized, right?" Rhi said sarcastically.

"Well, Hunter helped the police and now at least we know who was responsible. They'll be paying for it for sure," I said and then observed as the brand new window was being installed. "How much will this cost us?" I definitely didn't have many funds in my bank account. It was the whole reason I was in Hazelville in the first place.

"Don't worry about it. I paid for it from the store's budget."

"This day is getting better and better, isn't it?"

"So who threw that rock?"

"Oh, that detective refused to say. I don't know what he thought I'd do. Hunt them down myself?"

Rhi took a good look around the magic shop. "He was probably afraid you'd curse them or something."

"Really? He didn't seem to take any of this seriously when he was here."

"Most people are like that," Rhi said. "But at the end of the day, they'd rather be safe than sorry."

"Hmm, I didn't even think of that," I said. "I mean, it's not like I'm much of a witch anyway."

Rhi smiled. "You'll get there."

We watched as the men finished their work. Rhi gave them nice tips. They were nice enough, but I could see they were uncomfortable being in the shop. What was it with people and the occult? I myself always thought it would be cool to have magical powers, but I guess most people lived in fear of them.

"Where's grandma?" I asked when I remembered her sudden disappearance earlier.

"She should be around here somewhere," Rhi said.

Just then Rose made her appearance.

"What happened earlier?" I asked her.

"Hunter is a witch. He would have seen me and then our whole plan would go to hell."

"How is that?" I was genuinely curious what that would change.

"If he's responsible for my murder he'll know I'm still around. And if he suspects that I have any chance of remembering who killed me, who do you think he'll go after next?"

"Oh," I said when the realization finally hit.

"Exactly," Rose said. "I know you're new to all this, Rory, but you have to start thinking about these things."

"It's true," Rhi agreed. "We have to be careful around other witches. The Crowleys especially."

"I'm sorry," I said. "I just had a drink with him and he seemed like he was hiding something, but not something this big. I could be wrong, of course."

"In our world, being wrong could cost you your life," Rose said as she pointed out her see-through form. "Unless you're itching to join me in ghost land."

"I'm definitely not looking forward to that!" I said quickly.

Just then the doorbell chimed. The three of us

turned around to see who it was. Was it the detective? Hunter? A customer?

"Oh, it's just you," The three of us said in unison when we saw it was Scott.

"Thanks, guys," Scott said as he carried in a bag full of books.

"Found some goodies at Booked for Murder?"

He lifted the heavy bag. "You betcha. So how did your day go?" Just when he said that I noticed that the sun was starting to set. It would be dark soon.

"When do we close?" I asked Rhi.

"In an hour," she said.

"Good, because I don't want to be here too much longer. Can you drive Scott and me back or should we get a cab?"

"Sure, I can drive you guys back. It's no problem."

"Thanks," I said.

"Are you avoiding my question?" Scott said. "How was your little trip with that Hunter guy?"

I caught up Scott on what happened. I even told him about our little trip to the bar.

Scott looked at me with a curious look on his face. "You like him, don't you?"

"No," I said. "I just remembered who he was. It was nice to catch up. Plus, he's witch, too, and Rose made it pretty clear that he's not to be trusted. At least not for now."

"That sucks. You finally meet a guy and he might be a murderer. Just your luck."

"Thanks, Scott."

"You know I didn't mean it like that," he said as he set down his bag full of books. "What about that cute cop?"

"The one who refuses to investigate my grandmother's death?"

Rose nodded and so did Rhi.

"Fine, fine," Scott said. "You got me. But now that that little distraction is out of the way, don't you think it's time to finally see what's up in that attic?"

I had completely forgotten that before the rock smashed through our front window that all of us were in the back and I had a key in my hand to the mysterious door upstairs.

I took the key out of my purse. "I guess it's time to find out."

ELEVEN

I put the key in the lock.

"I told you, Rory, this is for your eyes only," my grandmother said again. "There's no need for Rhi, and especially Scott, to be here."

"Hey! I'm a person, too," Scott protested. "I might not be 'special' like you guys, but I've got feelings."

"I'm sure you do," Rose said. "Some things just aren't meant for mundanes."

"How does that work, anyway?" Scott asked. "If I wanted to, could I do some magic?"

"You have to have a talent for it. It's a hereditary trait. You could do mundane magic, which isn't very effective, especially when compared to what our magic can do."

"But Rory's mother and sister didn't seem to be magical at all," Scott pointed out.

"They have the potential for it," Rose explained. "They're just not interested."

"Are we going to open that door or not?" Rhi asked, looking at the end of her rope.

"Fine, fine," I said as I turned the key and opened the door wide.

I OPENED the door to the attic and saw a big empty space.

I don't know what I was expecting, but I wasn't expecting this. My grandmother had made such a big deal out of this secret room that I kind of thought it would be different. I entered the room and took a good look around. I saw cabinets against the walls. There was a small table in the middle of the room and a circle on the floor. It seemed that this was some kind of ritual room.

No one said anything, so I continued to look around. It was then that I noticed something peculiar about the room. The more I looked, the more I saw. There were certain objects, certain books even, that appeared and disappeared depending on which view I took of the room.

"Are you guys seeing this?" I asked my cousin and Scott.

"Seeing what? I'm only seeing a dusty old attic room. There's nothing special here!" Scott said.

"I gotta say I agree with Scott," Rhi said as she looked around the room. "I guess there's some kind of spell around the place and only you are able to see what's really up here."

"You guys really aren't seeing all of this?" I said as I approached a bookshelf that had different objects on it that kept disappearing and reappearing.

"Of course they can't see, this room wasn't meant for them. This room was only meant for you," my grandmother said.

"Well, this is disappointing," Scott said.

"Is there some way you could make us see what you're seeing?" My cousin asked.

"You've been a witch longer than I, haven't you?" I asked my cousin.

"I guess you have a point there," she said.

"It might weaken the protective barrier I have around this room if more than one person sees what's really here," Rose said.

Her words reminded me of something Hunter had said earlier. "What about the shop? Hunter said something about wards."

"Sadly, after I died the wards around the shop fell. Or were weakened at least," Rose said.

"I guess that makes sense, but why wasn't this room affected?" I asked.

"It was, the protection is a lot weaker here now, but it was a lot stronger when I was alive."

I walked around the room, careful not to touch any of the objects I saw out of the corner of my eye. Somehow I knew that I wasn't supposed to touch them. These were powerful objects, and I had no idea what any of them could do.

I looked at my grandmother with the question in my eyes, and she seemed to read my mind.

"Even I'm not sure what some of these objects do, but I do know that all of them are powerful in their own way."

"Well, this is boring," Scott said as he headed downstairs.

"I'm joining you," Rhi said as she followed him.

After they were gone my grandmother gave me a knowing look. "That's part of the spell too," she said. "Those who aren't allowed in here can't stay long even if they do manage to come in."

"That's kind of cool," I said.

I walked around the room, I even looked through the little window onto the street below.

"So what were you doing here on the day you died?" I asked my grandmother.

"If I knew the answer to that, I would probably know who killed me."

"I guess you're right," I said. "So is this some kind of ritual room or something?"

"Yes, I usually did spells here. This shop is built on a powerful nexus," she said. "Can't you feel it?"

"Not really. Am I supposed to?"

"Yes, but I suppose you haven't been a witch that long."

"Well, I did say I was willing to learn. So, when are the lessons going to start?"

"They've already started my dear granddaughter," Rose said as she flew around the room.

It was a strange sight seeing her see-through form flashing from one side of the room to the other. She seemed awfully interested in the objects on display, but when she tried to touch them, her hands went right through. She had a disappointed look on her face. Did she expect to be able to touch the objects?

"I guess you could show me how to reinforce the wards on this place," I said.

"Good idea, Rory, but you should probably ask Rhi for help, she knows more about this stuff than you do."

"Yeah, I'll ask her later."

I looked around the room some more, but to tell the truth, I was kind of disappointed. The way my grandmother kept talking about it I thought it was going to be cooler, but it was just a room in the attic with some special objects that I didn't even know what to do with.

It was getting dark outside so I decided it was time to go home. After all, that was where my grimoire was: the special spellbook that I had the sudden urge to open and hold in my hands and study from.

"Let's go home," I said.

I locked the door behind me and hoped that would be enough to protect what was on the other side.

TWELVE

LATER THAT NIGHT, JUST AS I FELL INTO A DEEP SLEEP, I was woken by a loud ringing.

It was the front door. I met Scott in the hallway.

"Who could it be at this hour?" I asked him.

"How should I know?"

Both of us went downstairs at the same time but thankfully Scott decided to open the door.

It was Detective Morgan on the other side of the door, and he didn't look happy.

"What are you doing here?" I asked, and then noticed that he was almost completely wet. It was raining outside.

"I'm afraid I'm not here under good circumstances," the detective said.

"What happened? Do you wanna come in?"

"I think it's better if we take this to the station," the detective said with a sad look in his eyes.

"What is this about? You can't just take her to the station without telling her why," Scott said, and this was the first time in our friendship that I was glad that he was such a mystery buff.

"I'm afraid the teenagers who vandalized your store earlier today have been found dead," the detective said. "And I have to ask you guys some questions."

"That's terrible! But you can't possibly think I had something to do with it?" I said, suddenly aware of the seriousness of the situation.

"It's standard procedure. If you didn't do anything you have nothing to fear," the detective said.

"Why can't you ask the questions here? It's the middle of the night."

"It wasn't my call," he said. By the look in his eyes, I could see that it actually wasn't. There was somebody above him, perhaps the local sheriff, who wanted to bring me, or us, in.

"Can I please put some proper clothes on?" I asked as I suddenly became aware that all I was wearing were my PJs and my hair was a mess.

"Yeah, just make it quick."

The detective waited in the living room, while Scott and I went upstairs to get dressed.

"This is crazy, first your grandmother and now this? I thought Hazelville was supposed to be a safe town!"

"I thought so too," I agreed. "But aren't most of those mysteries you read set in small towns, though?"

"You have a point there," he said. "But that's fiction! This is real life."

After we got dressed we solemnly followed the detective to his car. Scott and I sat in the backseat, but we didn't say much of anything.

I wanted to complain, and make light of the matter, but I just couldn't do it. I knew this was a serious matter. It seemed that two teenage boys were dead and earlier that day they had vandalized my store. I knew how it looked, but I couldn't possibly see how anyone would think I was involved. I had just gotten to town. Why would I go on a murder spree?

"How did they die?"

"We'll get to that later," the detective said as he looked on straight ahead. It was raining pretty heavily, and I guess he needed to keep his eyes on the road. But somehow I had a feeling that there was another reason he couldn't look me in the eye.

"Don't worry, Rory, it's going be alright," Scott tried to reassure me.

"Thanks," I said. "I just hope you're right."

Once we got to the station I saw a familiar face already there. He was sitting in the waiting room with an annoyed expression on his face. It was Hunter.

"So much for being a good citizen, am I right?" He said as he saw us approach.

"We'll get to you shortly, Mr. Crowley. But right now make sure to keep your comments to a minimum." The detective said as he led me to his office.

I saw him take a file from his desk, and then he told me to follow him. He opened the door to a small interrogation room. Oh crap, I was in real trouble now.

"Is this really necessary?" I asked, suddenly very nervous about the whole situation.

"If it wasn't, you wouldn't be here."

I sat down on the uncomfortable chair that the detective pointed out. "You want anything to drink? Coffee? Water? We might be here awhile," Detective Morgan asked as he opened the file.

"I guess water wouldn't hurt," I said, trying to buy myself some time to think. The detective took his file with him and returned a couple seconds later with a water bottle. I guess that was a bad idea. I opened the bottle and drank a little just to look normal.

"Where were you between 6 PM and 2 AM tonight?"

"We closed the shop around six, and then my cousin drove us home. It was just me and Scott from then on. We were at the house and we watched some TV. We had dinner and then both of us went to bed."

The detective was scribbling down notes. What was he writing? I wondered. What was there to write? It wasn't like I was involved in whatever happened, and I had a witness that I wasn't. Scott was with me the whole time. I just hoped that would be enough. Scott and I were strangers to this town, I knew that much. Plus, I owned a witch shop now and I knew that didn't go over well with some residents of the town.

"Thank you for your cooperation," he said. "Could you send Scott in next?"

"Sure," I said.

Scott was surprised to see me back so soon, and I have to say I was surprised myself.

I waited with Hunter in the waiting room. I saw Betty behind the reception desk with bags under her eyes. She did not look happy to be there, and when she looked our way there was a snide look in her eyes.

I ignored Betty and turned my attention to Hunter.

"Well that was strange," I said. "Did they ask you any questions yet?"

"No, not yet," he said. Hunter did not seem to be worried at all. At least I had Scott to corroborate my story, but as far as I knew Hunter had nobody.

"I can't believe they're dead," I said. "Do you have any idea who could've done it?"

"No, but I can tell you one thing: we're their number one suspects now."

I didn't like the sound of that. I had just gotten to town, and I did not need this. And to top it off my grandmother's ghost was asking me to solve her murder. The man next to me could very well be her killer, and here I was talking to him.

Scott returned. "You're next," he said to Hunter.

"Good luck," I said.

Hunter smiled. "I can take care of myself."

Scott stood above me. "Let's go home, I'm really tired."

"I wanna wait and see what Hunter has to say."

"Fine," Scott said as he sat next to me. "I wish I'd brought one of my books with me."

"Maybe you could think about your own book. How's that going anyway? Have you written anything since coming here?"

"Don't even ask," he said. It was clear that that was a touchy subject. I decided to drop it, and focus on the situation at hand.

"Do you think he had anything to do with it?"

"I doubt it," Scott said. "Why would he? He might have had the opportunity, but I don't see much of a motive."

"I guess you have a point there."

We waited in silence until Hunter returned.

"Don't leave town, Mr. Crowley," I heard the detective say to Hunter.

"What was that about?" I asked him.

"Apparently, I'm a person of interest. And I guess so are you guys." Hunter said and smiled.

I didn't feel like smiling. I'd only been in town barely three days, and I was already a murder suspect. A double murder suspect at that.

And to think, I left New York to get away from it all.

"I guess we should go home. It's pretty late," I said as I got up to go. Scott was by my side in no time. He looked sleepy, and I felt quite sleepy myself. All I wanted to do was crawl back into bed and forget that anything, that all of this, had happened.

"Well I guess I'll see you later," Hunter said. "I didn't plan on staying in town that long, but I guess I'll have to now that there's a double murder to solve. I just hope the good detective actually does his job and finds the persons or person responsible."

"I hope so too," I said. It was only when I watched Hunter ride off on his bike that I realized that Scott and I did not have a ride.

"Oh crap, should I go and call Rhi?"

I hated the idea of waking up my cousin, especially since it was so late.

"Just ask the detective to give us a ride back," Scott said. "After all, he was the one who dragged us here in the middle of the night."

"You have a point there." I headed back to the police station and found my way to the detective's office.

"We need a ride," I simply said.

The detective nodded. "I'm sorry about all this," he said apologetically. "If it was up to me, this could've been done back at your house, but the sheriff was adamant that we do this by the book."

"Well, what's done is done. I just wanna go back to bed now."

It was a quiet and quick drive back to the house. I waved goodbye to the detective as he drove off.

"He's cute," Scott said as we made our way up to the house. "But he definitely lost some points tonight."

"Oh definitely," I agreed. I locked the door behind us and hoped that would be enough to keep us safe for the night. After all, there was a killer out there. The killer who killed my grandmother, at least according to her, and the person who killed the two teenagers that had vandalized my shop earlier that day. I wondered why anybody would kill them? By the sound of what the detective had said about them, they seemed like petty criminals or troubled juveniles. Those usually didn't get murdered, did they?

"What happened?" Rose asked as she floated to where we were standing.

"It's a long story," I said. But when I saw the look on her face I proceeded to tell her the quick version.

"I wish they'd taken my murder that seriously," she said. "After you get to a certain age people start to treat you like you're invisible."

"Interesting choice of words," I said.

My grandmother made it a point to look through her see-through arms. "I guess it was," she said. "You get some sleep Rory, and we'll worry about this tomorrow. I'm a ghost now, so I guess I could poke around town and see if anybody knows anything."

"Can you do that?"

"I can try," she said with a concerned look on her face. "I have had trouble staying in certain places. The shop and this house are fine, but when I'm in other places, I start to lose focus. Being a ghost is not all it's cracked up to be."

I went upstairs to bed and resolved to worry about all of this tomorrow.

THIRTEEN

I was talking to my cousin in Book & Candle. It seemed that she was brought into the station a little after us.

"This is crazy," I said. "They can't possibly think that we are involved?"

"It's just normal procedure in a case like this," my cousin said.

"You seem awfully calm about the whole affair."

"Yeah, what's up with that?" Scott said as he browsed the book selection. "Are any of these books actually good?"

"Some are better than others," Rhi said. "As for the dead teenagers, yeah it's terrible, but none of us had anything to do with it."

"I guess you have a point there," I said.

"There's a killer out there," Rose said as she looked

through the window of the shop. "And he seems to be on a roll."

"It's probably completely unrelated to your death," Scott said.

"And how would you know?" Rose asked as she turned on Scott. She looked quite angry at the words he said to her.

"I mean, let's think about it. What kind of killer would kill an elderly woman, and then a couple of days later decide to kill a couple of teenagers? It just doesn't make much sense. I think these cases are completely unrelated."

"Maybe if you got your head out of those books once in a while you would know how the real world works," Rose said as she paced back and forth across the shop. It was strange seeing her float above the ground like that. I was still not used to having a ghost around.

"I wonder if there's any connection between what happened to them and what happened yesterday," Rhi said, as she powered up the laptop by the register.

"This place is really dead," I said. "There hasn't been a customer here since I arrived."

"I told you, most of our business is done online." My cousin said.

"Then why is there a physical location open at all?" I asked. "It just seems like a waste of money, doesn't it? You guys can save a lot on taxes by closing down the physical location and focusing on online sales."

"You will do no such thing," Rose said, suddenly very angry. "This shop has been open for twenty years. If I have anything to say about it, it will be open for at least twenty more."

"I'm sorry, I was just trying to be realistic here."

"I gotta agree with Rory," Scott said. "Do you know how many small businesses go under each year? This place will fold eventually. It's better to cut your losses now than wait for it to become a liability later."

"I'm starting to rethink my decision to leave my shop to you," my grandmother told me as she gave Scott the stink eye.

"I wasn't saying I was going to sell it, I was just saying it makes more sense."

"This shop was built on a nexus of power," my cousin reminded me. "If we close shop, or tried to sell this property, another witch would just come along and take it from us. And then our online sales will dry up anyway. Plus, we have our busy seasons. You should see us around Halloween time. There're so many people there's usually a line outside."

"I'm sure there is, but that doesn't mean anything if the rest of the year is this dead."

"Sorry," I said to my grandmother when I realized what I had just said.

"Don't be silly, I know I'm dead. I've already made my peace with it, I just wish you would get on solving my murder so I could just move on already."

My grandmother seemed frustrated and I couldn't blame her. But I wasn't sure what she was expecting from me exactly. It wasn't like I was a detective or anything.

"Your grandmother has a point," Scott said as he joined us by the counter.

"Thank you, Scott," Rose said, suddenly acting like Scott was her favorite person in the world.

"What do you mean?" I asked Scott.

"I think we should focus on solving the murders of the teenagers, and maybe that will lead us back to Rose's killer. There's bound to be more clues in their case anyway."

"Good thinking, young man," my grandmother said.

Scott seemed proud of himself. He liked the attention and approval he was getting from my grandmother. I rolled my eyes at them and wondered what exactly was wrong with the world today. I wished that I'd never answered that phone call. I wished that I had just stayed in New York and kept on waitressing. At least back there nobody expected me to solve murders like it was my job.

"That's a good idea, Scott," Rhi said as she looked up from the laptop.

"Have all of you lost your minds?" I asked the three of them. Well, I knew my grandmother wanted me to solve her murder, but now my cousin and my best friend seemed excited by the prospect of solving a double murder that had just happened. Not to mention that we were persons of interest in the case because of what the victims did to our shop.

"I think I found something," Rhi said as she looked at her laptop.

I was by her side in no time and so were Scott and Rose. We all looked down on the screen to see what she was talking about.

It was a story about the murder of the teenagers.

"Does it say anything about how they died?" Scott asked.

Rhi scrolled down the page then proceeded to read the tiny letters.

"Doesn't really say," she said. "I guess they're trying to keep the information private for now."

"That's what they usually do," Scott said. "The police in the mystery books and thrillers I've read. They'll probably reveal the cause of death in a day or two. After they've asked everybody questions, waiting for somebody to slip up information that hasn't been released to the press yet."

"That seems like highly sophisticated thinking for a small town like Hazelville," I said.

"But remember, Detective Morgan hails from Chicago," Scott reminded me. "Maybe he's using the methods he used back in the big city over here."

"If so, God help us," I said. Just then the bell chimed and all four of us turned to the door. It was just a delivery boy with a couple of boxes.

"Oh, hi Bobby," Rhi said. "Is that our shipment of candles? We've been waiting for those for over a week now."

"Yeah, they just arrived," Bobby said.

My cousin signed the paper and gave it back to Bobby. I noticed that Bobby seemed quite taken by my cousin, but Rhi didn't seem to notice at all. I'd have to talk to her about it later.

"Did you guys hear about the murders?"

"Unfortunately, yes. We heard it from the detective on the case." Rhi said.

"Oh wow, how so?" Bobby asked, genuinely curious.

"Apparently, we're the prime suspects," Rhi said and rolled her eyes.

"We are persons of interest," Scott corrected her. "If we were prime suspects, that would mean that the police had something on us to connect us to the crime. They have no such thing."

"Let's hope it stays that way," my cousin said.

"Well I gotta be on my way," Bobby said. "I've still got a couple of deliveries to make."

We said goodbye to Bobby and then returned to our regularly scheduled programming.

I WASN'T at all sure about what I was doing, but I knew it was the only way to make any headway in our search for Rose's killer.

"I'll be a watch out," Scott said as he shifted nervously.

"Thanks," I said as I rolled my eyes.

So where were we exactly that made Scott so nervous? We were at the police station. That's right, the last place a person of interest should be.

Rhi, Rose, Scott and I all agreed that this had to be done.

Rhi was out in the parking lot, doing a little looking out of her own. We'd waited for over two hours in front waiting for Detective Morgan's car to drive out of that parking lot.

"Maybe we should have thought this through better," Rhi had said, as she looked on impatiently. "Maybe we should have created an emergency…"

"That's crazy," I had told her, but I couldn't help but think the same thing. Maybe if we set off some alarm in town we wouldn't have been stuck there waiting for the detective to leave.

Thankfully, after about fifteen minutes we finally saw the detective leave. As he looked around suspiciously all three of us ducked inside the car.

So here we were now. This was the plan. I took a deep breath as I approached the reception desk. Betty, the receptionist, looked about as receptive as ever.

"What do you want?" She asked as she put down a thick romance novel that she apparently just started reading.

"I'm here to see Detective Morgan," I said.

Betty raised her eyebrows. "And why would you need to see him?"

"I lost an earring in his office yesterday," I said, trying to look as worried as possible.

"And that's my problem because...?"

"Can you just call the detective and tell him I need to look around his office. Maybe he found it? Did he mention anything?" I lifted up an antique-looking earring from my pocket. "It looks like this," I explained. Betty's drawn on eyebrows went up even higher. "It belonged to my grandmother..."

Betty rolled her eyes. "Well, you're out of luck young lady. The detective just left for lunch."

"Damn," I said, trying to look really bummed about the whole situation.

"You're free to take a seat and wait," Betty offered and I thanked her as I walked back to where Scott was.

"There's no way we're getting in there while she's here," I said as I sat down next to him.

"I told you that you should have just talked to the detective," Scott said.

"You're delusional," I said. "He thinks I'm a murderer."

"He's smitten with you. It's been obvious since he laid his eyes on you."

"Stop."

"It's true," Scott said. "I'll go back and tell Rhi the

situation and you stay here and wait for the detective. Then use your womanly charms to distract him while you look for clues."

I rolled my eyes. "Yeah, I'm sure that's gonna go over well."

Scott got up to go and I joined him.

"Rory, you've got to stay here and play the part of the damsel in distress. Just call us when you need a ride, okay?"

I hated Scott in that moment. "Fine," I said.

I took my phone out and surfed the net, trying to kill some time. I jumped a little when I noticed a large figure standing over me. When I looked up I saw that it was the detective.

"Detective Morgan," I said,

"Call me Jack. Everyone does," he said.

This was going to be easier than I thought.

I tried to look as innocent as possible as I put my phone away and took out the earring. I explained the situation to him. He didn't seem convinced, but I saw a hint of a smile at the corner of his lips.

"Follow me," he said and I did.

He took me to the interrogation room first. "You were here the longest," he said as he opened the door for me. "It probably fell somewhere here."

I stifled a groan. This was not going the way I pictured it at all. I pretended to look around but obviously found no sign of the earring. "It must be in your office, unless I lost it somewhere else entirely," I offered and immediately regretted my words. Here I was trying to convince him that I'd lost an earring in his office while at the same time coming up with a scenario where I didn't.

Jack smiled as he led me to his office. He unlocked the door with his key.

Yet another reason Scott was right that I needed Jack here.

"Be quick," he said as he put a couple of files down on his desk.

I nodded as I looked around as slowly as possible. I nearly jumped out of my skin when the phone rang.

Jack answered. "What does he want?" he said to the person on the other end, probably Betty. "I'll be right there. I'm coming, calm down."

"I'll be back in a minute. Behave yourself," he said as he left.

As soon as he was out of sight I immediately went to his desk and leafed through the files. I finally found the one on the dead teenagers.

I gasped as I read all the gory details of their deaths. Then I saw an underlined, handwritten note, probably by Jack.

Brakes were tampered with.

A chill went through me.

What kind of person would want these two teenage boys to die in such a horrific manner?

I quickly put the files back where I found them and took out the second earring I had in my pocket.

I walked back to the reception desk. "I found it," I announced to Betty and Jack.

Jack barely noticed that I was even there. He was having a very heated conversation with another familiar figure. Hunter.

"What are you doing here?" Hunter asked me.

"I could ask you the same thing," I shot back but lifted the earring as an answer anyway.

"I don't remember you wearing those earrings yesterday," Hunter said and I knew he was trying to piss me off.

"They were probably hidden by my hair," I quickly said.

"Yeah, I guess so," Hunter said.

"As fun as this is," Jack said, "I think you two should go. Mr. Crowley, for the last time, stay in town or I'll be forced to put out an APB, understand?"

Hunter nodded but didn't seem happy about it at all.

"Thanks for letting me look," I said to Jack. "I don't know what I would have done without your help."

"Glad to be of service," Jack said and smiled.

"You didn't really lose that earring, did you?" Hunter said as the doors closed behind us.

"Of course not. Do you think I'm that stupid?"

"Apparently Detective Morgan thinks so."

I punched him in the arm lightly. "That's not very nice. The real question is what you were doing there?"

"I ran into your friend and cousin and decided to lend a hand by offering a distraction."

"Oh, thanks," I said.

"No problem. But I did do it under one condition."

"I'm not going out on a date with you," I quickly said.

Hunter laughed. "You have a very high opinion of yourself, don't you?"

"If I don't, who will?"

"I guess you've got a point there. No, I want to know what you found out."

I didn't say anything for over a minute as we stood by Hunter's bike.

"I can go back in and find out for myself," Hunter warned.

"Really? And how would you do that?" I asked.

"Magic, of course."

"Fine," I said. For some reason, I didn't like the idea of Hunter using some kind of magic on Jack. What? He seemed like a nice guy. He even helped me find my earring.

I told Hunter about how the breaks were tampered with.

"That's awful," he said. "Sure, they weren't valedictorians, but I don't think they deserved to die for what they did."

I nodded. "Well, thanks for the help but I've gotta

go," I said as I took out my cell. I hoped Scott and Rhi weren't too far away.

"I can give you a ride back," Hunter offered as he took the extra helmet and held it out for me.

It was tempting, but in the end, I decided against it. I had to go back to the shop and I definitely didn't want him scaring off Rose's ghost.

"Thanks, but I'll be okay. Have a nice day, Hunter."

FOURTEEN

"I can't believe you guys told Hunter that I was at the police station snooping around."

"I said no such thing," Rhi said. She made it a point to look in Scott's direction.

"I'm sorry, it seemed like a good idea at the time," Scott said.

"You thought sending what could possibly be my murderer to where my granddaughter was was a good idea?" My grandmother said as she floated up and down.

"It worked, didn't it?" Scott said. "And I don't think Hunter had anything to do with your murder."

"If you met his family, you'd think otherwise," Rhi offered.

"The Crowleys have always hated the Wiltzs," Rose chimed in.

"I've gotta agree with Scott," I said.

"You what?" My grandmother said as both she and Rhi looked at me with shock on their faces.

"He seems nice enough. I don't think he's capable of murder."

Rose flew away in a rage until she was out of sight.

"Look what you've done now," Rhi admonished me. "You made grandma mad."

"Why is no one focusing on the fact that at least we have a cause of death now?" Scott said.

Rhi rolled her eyes. "We're not cops," she said. "We should be focusing on granny's murder and I say Hunter Crowley is our number one suspect."

With that, Rhi left and joined Rose in the back.

I sighed. "I should have never come here," I said to Scott.

"Its's gonna be okay. You're doing the right thing. You have to follow the evidence, not prejudices."

"Let's go back home," I said. "I'm sure Rhi can handle this wasteland on her own."

"You wanna look through that magic book, don't you?" Scott said.

"How'd you know?"

"'Cause that's exactly what I'd wanna do if I had a strange book at home that only I could read."

Rhi let us borrow her car, with a promise that we'd come and pick her up in a couple of hours.

"Are you coming along?" I asked Rose as we turned to leave.

"I'll stay here awhile and watch over your cousin," Rose said.

"Is she in any danger?" I asked, suddenly very worried. The teenagers who had vandalized our shop were dead.

"Just in case," Rose explained.

"Don't worry, Rory," Rhi said. "I can take care of myself. I'm a witch, remember?"

I nodded. I wanted to say that grandma was a witch, too, but held back.

"See you later," was all I said as Scott and I left.

It felt strange leaving that shop without Rhi in tow.

Once we got home, it was four in the afternoon and I felt like I'd ran a marathon for some reason.

"Want some tea?" Scott offered.

"You know me so well."

I went up to the attic to get the grimoire. Once I returned to the living room the tea was already waiting for me and there even some cookies on a plate.

"This is why I love you," I said as I took a bite of a delicious cookie. Then I proceeded to dip it in my tea.

Scott took the grimoire out of my hands and flipped through the pages. Pretty soon he became cross-eyed trying to read it.

"I wonder if there's a spell you can do to make it

readable for me. You did one that let me see your grand-mother's ghost."

"There probably is," I agreed. "I wish I actually knew half this stuff. Hell, even less than half would be nice. Neither Rhi or grandma have found the time to teach me anything."

I took the book back and flipped through the pages. Formulas, incantations, and long-winded rituals all made their appearance and I didn't know the first thing about how they would actually work.

"Huh," I found myself saying when I saw the head-line of one page.

"What is it?" Scott said, putting down the paperback he was reading.

"It's a love potion," I said. "I guess that part wasn't a myth."

Scott seemed excited by the prospect. "Do it!"

"What? I'm not going to cast a love spell on unsus-pecting mundanes. That's just wrong. Even I know that much."

"If it was wrong, would it be in your grandmother's personal spellbook?" Scott asked.

"It's probably a family recipe or something. I mean, back in the day, when women needed to find husbands to survive in the world, I can see how it would be useful. But now? It just seems manipulative."

"Think about it, Rory," Scott said. I knew exactly what that look meant. He was about to go on and on playing devil's advocate when he knew that I was right and that he agreed with me.

"Please don't," I warned him.

Scott ignored me and took a sip of his tea for good measure, presumably to prepare his throat for the rant that was about to be unleashed.

"You say love spells are manipulative, but if you think about it, they're just another tool in the modern arsenal. Why should people with good looks get all the advantage? Love spells are just another way to even the playing field. If you're good looking and rich, you've already got plenty to choose from. Those of us who aren't need something a little extra, and if that comes in the form of a love potion or spell or whatever, why is that any worse than all the other things that attract people to each other?"

"You know exactly why," I said. "Because you'd be taking the free will of the person away."

"I hate it when you make too much sense," Scott said and went back to reading his book.

I kept flipping through the book trying to find anything useful to the situation we were in. My main objective was to find out who had killed the teenage boys and go from there.

"This might work..." I said more to myself than to Scott as I pulled the book closer.

"What is it? A money spell that ends in an inheritance from a dead relative?" Scott offered.

I gave him the stinkiest stink eye I could.

"Oh, right, sorry," he quickly said.

"No, it's a tracking spell," I said.

"And who are we trying to track?"

"The killer of course." I read through the entry. "Crap, we're gonna need something from the murder weapon."

Scott's eyes suddenly became wide. And then a smile appeared across his face. "The car."

"Yes," I said. "We'll have to wait for the cover of night to go. What time is it?"

"Crap, it's fifteen to six," Scott said.

"We've gotta pick up Rhi," I said as I went up to get my jacket. The sun was going to set soon and it was going to be dark out. I doubted that Rhi wanted anything to do with our plan, so I decided not to tell her anything.

Rhi drove us back home and it seemed like she'd calmed down since our last encounter.

Once we were home, Scott and I dusted off Rose's old and beat up car. We took it out of the garage and let it air out a little.

"And where exactly are the two of you going?" Rose demanded to know when she saw the car.

"We'll tell you later," I quickly said as we got the hell out of there.

"She'll have to know eventually," Scott said as he took the wheel.

"I know. I'm just not in the mood for that conversation right now."

I kept checking my phone. "The junkyard should be this way," I offered even though I had no idea where exactly we were. Scott didn't have a great sense of direction, either.

It took us about an hour to find the junkyard when it should have taken no more than fifteen minutes.

Scott parked by a side road and turned off the engine. "Did you bring the bolt-cutters?"

"Did you?" I spat back.

"It was a genuine question," Scott said in his defense.

"I'm sure it was. You just thought of the bolt-cutter when you saw that fence, am I right?"

Scott looked guilty as charged.

"We wouldn't make good criminals, would we?" I said.

"Or amateur sleuths," Scott added.

After several minutes of looking miserable and making sure that nobody else was around, we finally found the courage to get out of the car.

It was chilly and I immediately tightened my jacket around me. "Maybe this was a bad idea," I said.

Scott looked up at the night sky. "It's almost a full moon," he said. "And you're a witch. Isn't that supposed to be a special thing for you guys?"

"I think you're thinking of werewolves," I offered.

"I'm pretty sure it's witches too."

I rolled my eyes. "Let's just see if we can even get into this place. If that car is even here."

"I checked online. This is where they bring all the wrecks."

"I'm not sure I want to see *this* wreck. Those teenagers died in that car..."

Scott drew closer and put a hand on my shoulder. "It has to be done," he simply said and I knew he was right.

We made our way to the big doors. Of course, there was a lock and chains.

"We could try climbing over?" Scott offered.

"Is that what the characters in your books do?"

"Only the great ones," Scott said and grinned.

I looked up at the wire fence. The top of it was not spiked, thankfully, but it still didn't look safe enough to touch with bare hands. I took off my jacket.

"I guess we could try climbing over," I offered.

Scott nodded as he proceeded to take his own jacket off.

It took a couple of tries but eventually I managed to get my jacket on top of the fence. Scott boosted me up and I climbed up.

When I was at the top of the fence I made the mistake of looking down and almost fell.

"I hate heights," I said as I tried to hold on for dear life.

"Don't be such a baby," Scott said. "Just lower yourself down slowly and then drop when you can't go any lower."

I did as I was told and eventually found myself on the ground. The fall was more painful than even I anticipated. I hated gravity.

Scott was next and to my dismay he was much faster and his fall was far more graceful than mine.

We put our jackets back on and went in search of the car.

Looking around at all the wrecked cars around us, I wasn't sure it was going to be such an easy task. And then I heard voices in the distance.

"Did you hear that?" I asked Scott and he nodded.

We kept to the shadows and were as quiet as the dead as we followed the sounds of the voices.

Then something peculiar happened. I saw the source of the voices. Then I saw the wrecked car they were standing next to.

The two teenage boys were arguing about something.

It took me a moment to realize that both of them were see-through, just like Rose.

"I guess we found it," I said as I pointed out the scene to Scott.

We approached the two of them, careful not to scare them off.

"You were the one driving, Boyd, it's your fault."

"Nah, Nathan, it's yours. You distracted me with that shitty music."

The two ghostly figures turned around at the same time when they noticed me and Scott approaching.

"Who the hell are you?" Boyd asked us.

Nathan rolled his eyes. "Probably some goth freaks. Go to the cemetery, losers!"

I looked down at my all-black clothes. Then I looked at Scott, who had a dark brown jacket on which might look black in the dark.

"Why go to the cemetery when the ghosts are here?" I said as I approached the two youths.

The two of them looked at each other. "What the hell are you talking about?" Boyd said. He had long greasy blond hair and a permanent scowl on his face. Nathan had a short military cut and much the same expression.

"You guys are dead is what she's trying to say," Scott said tactfully.

"You two better get the hell out of here before I make you," Nathan said as he approached us, his hands turned to fists.

Boyd followed his friend's lead.

Scott and I stood our ground.

The two youths tried to push us out of the way acting all macho, but instead just went through us. The looks on their faces were priceless.

"Is this a joke?" Boyd asked no one in particular.

I sighed. "You're dead, get over it."

While I didn't approve of their murders, I did not have much sympathy for the two youths. They were bullies who liked to push people around, and not to mention they had no problem vandalizing my store. What if I had been standing by the window when they threw that rock? I would have been the ghost now. So no, I did not have much patience for their shenanigans.

"But we can't be. We'd be in heaven or something right?" Nathan offered, a confused look on his face.

Both Scott and I laughed in unison.

"Heaven? Think a little lower," I offered. I myself wasn't sure if heaven and hell even existed. Rose was very mysterious about the whole thing.

"Hey! That's not nice," Boyd complained. "I had so much to live for..."

"Me too," Nathan agreed.

Suddenly the two youths looked pretty bummed out and I couldn't help but feel sorry for them.

"We're wasting time," Scott reminded me. "We came here for a reason, and it wasn't to talk to these losers."

Nathan and Boyd turned on Scott. If looks could kill, Scott would have been a ghost right about now.

"You vandalized her shop!" Scott said in his defense.

"Oh, that was your place?" Nathan asked. He looked almost apologetic.

"Yes," I said. "But that's not why we're here. We're trying to figure out who killed you guys."

"Somebody killed us? Why? How?" Boyd asked.

"Yeah, I guess they cut your breaks," I said.

"I told you it wasn't my fault," Boyd said to Nathan, who shrugged his shoulders in response.

"I need a part of your car for a spell I'm doing." I offered.

The two youths looked at each other then back at me and Scott.

"I want nothing to do with witches," Boyd said.

"Neither do I," Nathan agreed.

The two youths started to back away slowly.

I rolled my eyes.

"Really?" I said.

"They're scared of you," Scott offered.

"We're not afraid," the two boys said in unison.

"Well, why don't you come here and tell us that?" I said as I crossed my arms.

The two teenagers stayed where they were.

I took a deep breath. "Do you guys have any idea who's responsible for your deaths?"

The two teenagers exchanged knowing looks but didn't utter a word.

"Fine," I said. "I'll just get what I came for and be on my way then." Dealing with one ghost was more than enough for me, and I wasn't looking forward to adding two more to the mix.

Scott observed the ghosts as I took a piece of the car the two youths were driving when they died. It was pretty easy picking out a piece since the car was basically falling apart.

"That's our ride you're wrecking!" Boyd complained as he suddenly joined me.

"Really? We're in a junkyard right now."

Boyd looked around. "I guess you have a point there."

FIFTEEN

"THAT WAS SOMETHING," SCOTT SAID AS HE DROVE US back to the house. I held the piece of the car I had taken and hoped that it would be enough.

We needed a clue, any clue, as to who was responsible and this seemed like the best way to move ahead. I just hoped that my grandmother would understand.

When we entered through the front door, Rose was there as expected with her arms crossed and a question on her face.

"What exactly are you planning, Rory?" She asked me.

I showed her the piece of the car.

"What is that?" Rose asked.

I explained it to her and saw the look on her face. She was not happy at all.

"It's the only way," I said as Scott and I headed up to the attic.

Not surprisingly, Rose was right on our tail.

I set the piece of the car down on the small table in the middle of the attic and I opened the spell book to the page I'd marked earlier.

"This is a tracking spell," I explained.

"I know what it is. I've been a witch far longer than you, my child."

"Will you help us then?" I asked her.

Rose nodded. "Of course."

Rose helped me find all the right herbs I needed. We lit some candles for ambiance. Rose guided me into trance with her voice as Scott observed from a relative distance.

"Repeat these words as you focus on the link," my grandmother said and I followed her instructions to a T, though I had to repeat the strange sounds a couple of times before I got them right.

"Wow," I heard Scott say and I opened my eyes to see why. Then I saw it: the piece of the car was glowing with power.

"Pick it up," my grandmother urged me.

I did as I was told and was astonished by what happened next. The piece of metal felt hot in my hands, but that was not the strange part. The light that had illuminated it earlier turned into a beacon of sorts, pointing in the direction of the window.

"Great job," my grandmother said. "That line of light will lead you to the one responsible."

"What if someone sees it?" I asked her.

"Don't worry about it. Mundanes won't see it at all, at least not without some help," Rose said as she looked in Scott's direction.

It was fairly late at night, but Scott and I decided that it was now or never. Rose agreed, saying that the spell would wear off if we waited too long.

As Scott drove and I held the piece of metal, I felt a strange sensation throughout my entire body. Was this how it felt to do magic? To be magic? I wondered why my mother had rejected the whole notion and refused to let her daughters in on the secret. Did she even know what she was missing?

"Take a left there," I said as the light suddenly changed direction.

Scott was awfully quiet so I decided to ask him about it.

"I'm just trying to get used to the weirdness," was all he said. I noticed that he kept looking back at the object in my hands. He'd seen ghosts and this was too weird for him?

We took several more turns before the light focused in on one thing. It was the local inn.

Scott and I looked at each other. Neither of us said what we were thinking. We just got out of the car.

I took the piece of metal in my hands and let it guide

us further. We entered the inn and the light led us to the back, the dining area that had a small bar.

The light shone on one person sitting alone at the bar with a drink in his hand.

It was Hunter.

BY THE LOOK on Scott's face, I could see that he thought that this wasn't a good idea.

I ignored his reservations. I told him to stand back so that I had a chance to speak to Hunter alone.

I sat down next to him.

He smiled that devilish smile. Then he noticed the thing in my hand and the light pointing straight at him.

"Oh," he said.

"Yeah. You've got an explanation for me?"

"Well, first I'd like to know what that thing is."

"It's part of a car that the juveniles drove. I did a spell to track down the person responsible for their deaths."

"Oh," Hunter said. "And it led you to me?" He took a large sip of his drink, finishing it off.

"That's all you've got to say?"

"Would you believe me if I said that I was innocent?"

"Probably not," I said. "But it wouldn't hurt to hear the words anyway."

"Rory, I'm not responsible for their deaths. I'd never do such a thing. I know your family doesn't like mine, but that doesn't mean that I go around killing people for no reason."

"And how do you explain this?" I lifted the thing to his face.

Hunter put a hand over his eyes. "You can turn that thing off now," he said.

"How?"

"May I?"

I reluctantly handed him the piece. I saw the look on Scott's face across the room. But what did I have to lose? The spell had already led me to him. It wasn't like I could use it as evidence against him or anything.

Hunter held his hand over the piece of metal and uttered some words. I recognized a few from the spell casting earlier.

The piece of metal stopped glowing. There was no magic in it now.

I held it in my hands. "I'll have to tell Jack," I finally said.

"The detective?"

"Yeah."

"And what are you going to tell him exactly? That you're a witch and that you cast a spell to find the murderer and it led you to me?"

Well, when he put it like that...

I got up from the chair. "This isn't over," I said as I turned to go.

"Rory," Hunter called back and I turned around reluctantly. "Be careful."

I wasn't sure if I should have taken that as a friendly warning or as an outright threat. In the end, I decided that it was a bit of both.

"Are you freaking crazy?" Scott wasn't happy with me when we exited the inn, with as many questions as we entered it.

"I had to give him a chance to explain," I said.

"All you did was tip him off that we were onto him," Scott said as he unlocked the car.

After he opened the door for me, I slid back into the passenger seat. I looked back at the inn and the now useless piece of metal in my hands. I had to set it down. I could no longer either look at it or touch it.

"I TOLD YOU HE WAS RESPONSIBLE," Rhi said.

"I'm not so sure," I said.

"Rory? Really?" Scott said as he leafed through a paperback in the corner of Book & Candle.

"Magic doesn't lie," Rhi said. "The spell led you to Hunter, that means Hunter is the guilty party."

"He told me he wasn't, and I believe him."

"Just because you find the guy hot doesn't mean he's innocent," Scott said.

"I agree with Scott," Rhi said. "I mean he is hot, but that doesn't mean he's not evil!"

"There was just something different about him, something that makes me believe him. I don't know what it is, and I might be completely wrong, but until we have good hard evidence, I will not convict the guy."

I wasn't even sure myself if what I was saying made much sense. Maybe Hunter was guilty, who knows? I just had a feeling that he wasn't. The way he told me that he wasn't guilty, it just felt like he was telling me the truth.

The bell chimed and all three of us immediately looked at the door. Book & Candle did not have a lot of customers so it was a surprise to find somebody that actually came through the front door.

But when I saw who it was, I froze in place, almost forgetting how to breathe.

"Rory, Scott, I'm here to talk to you guys." Detective Jack Morgan said as he entered the shop. Rhi gave us a look and I told her with a look of my own that it was alright. She took the hint and proceeded to go into the back, though I was sure she was eavesdropping.

"What's this about, detective?" I asked as I pretended like I was looking at something profoundly interesting on the laptop computer in front of me.

"I'm here to talk to you guys about what you did last night," Jack said as he ran his hand through his hair, looking tired and beat up. Detective Jack Morgan did not look like he'd gotten a lot of sleep last night.

"We were at home at my grandmother's house," I

said. I observed as the look on the detective's face changed from frustrated to angry to frustrated again.

"I have it on good authority that you guys were at the local junkyard yesterday."

"And what authority would that be?"

"We have a surveillance camera showing you and your friend here late at night doing God knows what, and then it clearly showed you taking something from the vehicle that caused the wreck that killed the two teenagers the other day. Can you explain any of this? Especially the part where you guys look like you're talking to air. That was the part that caused especial ruckus in our police department."

Well, that was a lot to take in. If only Scott and I had thought about the surveillance cameras. But in a small town like Hazelville, who would've thought that they would have such things. I certainly didn't notice any when we were going there, but I guess I wasn't really looking for any anyway.

"Oh, well, I guess we were out for a walk yesterday?" I asked as I looked in Scott's direction. Scott was having none of it. He looked guilty as hell and no matter what I said the detective would know that I was lying.

"You just happened to take a walk to the local junkyard where we kept the wrecked car from the accident that killed two people? The very two people that vandalized your shop recently. You also happened to climb the fence into the junkyard and you found the car and took a piece of it with you. Oh, and you acted weirdly like you were talking to somebody there. And I missing anything?"

"No, that's about it," Scott said as he looked up from the book he was leafing through.

"Well, none of that really proves anything, does it?" I said as I looked anywhere but at the detective.

"I can charge you with tampering with evidence in an ongoing investigation."

"I did no such thing! I was trying to help..."

"What my cousin is trying to say is that it's none of your business. If you have any more questions, you can contact our lawyer."

I looked up as Rhi entered the room. She seemed awfully confident.

"I don't think there's a lawyer in the world who will be able to get you guys out of this one. It's best that you tell me everything or I'll be forced to take you into the station right now."

"On what charge?" Rhi asked.

"Obstruction of justice, tampering with evidence in an ongoing investigation, take your pick."

"That won't be necessary, Detective," Scott said as he joined us by the counter.

"Are you ready to talk?"

"It was my idea," Scott said. "I just wanted to see the car. I'm sort of a mystery buff if you haven't noticed." Scott lifted up the paperback mystery he had just been leafing through. The detective looked at him like he was crazy.

"Yeah, what he said," I said, sending a telepathic *"thank you"* to Scott.

"And what exactly were you guys planning on doing?"

"We were just snooping around," Scott said. "I just wanted to see if we could find anything that would clear our names. We were definitely not responsible for what happened to those teenagers, and I just wanted to make sure we had the evidence to prove it."

"You do know it's against the law to tamper with evidence?"

"Of course," Scott said and sighed. "But if you guys really needed it for anything you would have chosen a much safer place to put the car."

"Really?" Jack rolled his eyes. He was annoyed, that much was certain.

"I know I was wrong now, but you have to admit you didn't leave us much choice," Scott said.

"And what about the piece of the car you took?"

"We can return it to you," I quickly said.

"You guys realize that your actions last night have made you look more guilty than ever, don't you?" The detective asked, looking like he was disappointed in us. I found that strange, wasn't he the one who thought we did it in the first place? Oh wait, that was the sheriff. We still hadn't seen the sheriff around and I was starting to wonder if he even existed.

"Rory, give him back the piece we took," Scott said.

"Sure," I said as I reached down below the counter and took hold of the object. I handed it to the detective.

Jack looked it over suspiciously, and then when he didn't see anything too strange about it, he pocketed the small piece of the car.

"This doesn't change anything," Jack said. "You two are in a lot of trouble."

"Detective, either charge them or be on your way," Rhi said, looking tougher than ever. I was surprised by her abrasive demeanor toward the detective. After all, he had the power to arrest us. And it wasn't like Scott and I could get out of this easily. They had the video of us doing the deed.

"Can I talk to you privately?" Jack asked me as he glanced from Scott to Rhi. It seemed he wasn't a fan of Rhi's attitude toward him, and I couldn't say I blamed the guy.

"Sure," I said reluctantly. I found myself saying that a lot in his presence.

Scott and Rhi took the message and decided to make themselves scarce.

"I'm not going to turn you in," Jack said when they were gone.

"And why is that?" I was genuinely curious. I thought for sure that the good detective was going to haul me and Scott off to jail, especially after Rhi's little display.

"Look, I lied before. I did not show the video to any of the others at the office. I decided to come here first to see if you guys have a good explanation. It looks like you don't."

"Scott already said why," I tried to act normal, but apparently Jack could see right through me. Maybe there was a reason that acting dream of mine didn't work out...

"Really? It might have sounded convincing coming from him, but it doesn't from you. Why were you guys really there?" Jack seemed calmer now than when he'd arrived, but he still looked a little on edge. I noticed that he looked around nervously as if at any moment something would jump out at him.

I knew exactly what he didn't want to hear, and what he did want to hear at the same time. They were the same thing.

"Witch stuff," I simply said.

"Witch stuff?" Jack looked incredulous. "What exactly is your definition of 'witch stuff'?" He looked around the shop again, with more attention to detail this time.

"I thought it would be a good idea to try a tracking spell to find the killer," I said.

Jack was at a loss for words.

I knew he didn't know what to make of my admission, and that's exactly why I made it. Jack didn't believe in magic, so what was the harm in telling him the truth?

"So you really believe in...all of this?" Jack motioned around the shop with his hands.

"So what if I do?"

"It's just, well, I'm sorry, but I didn't think you were the kind of person who would take any of this seriously."

I sighed. "I didn't. I don't. I don't know. Ever since I came back to town, my world has turned upside down a little."

I was surprised at how open I was with him. I barely knew the guy and here I was bearing my soul to him.

Jack didn't know what to say to that. "Stay out of trouble," he finally said as he turned to go. He opened the door but turned back one final time. "I don't know if I'll be able to protect you next time."

With that, Jack was gone. In the next moment, Scott and Rhi were on my case. Rhi looked especially pissed.

"I can't believe you told him the truth. He's a cop!"

"It worked, didn't it? And it's not like he actually believed me."

"And what if he happened to be a witch hunter?"

"There are witch hunters? What is this the dark ages?" I joked, but Rhi's face remained serious.

"This is not a joke, Rory," she said carefully. "There's a lot more to the world than you realize, and not all of it is pleasant."

I didn't like her condescending tone. Sure, she knew more about this witch stuff than me, but there was no need for her to talk to me like I was a child.

"I'm sorry, I didn't know that was even a thing," I finally said, trying not to cause a scene, even though I had the strong urge to start pulling hair.

"Well, it is," Rhi said after she calmed down a bit.

I couldn't let it go that easily, though. "Don't you think owning an occult shop kind of negates the whole secret witch thing?"

"You have a point there," Scott agreed.

"There's plenty of occult shops in the world. Very few of them are owned by witches of our kind. Plus, those of us that are real have protections and the witch hunters know that. Coming to our turf would give us the advantage, and believe me they don't want that."

I found that interesting. "And what kind of witches are we?" I was genuinely curious.

"The supernatural kind."

SIXTEEN

ROSE WASN'T HAPPY WITH ME EITHER. RHI HAD DECIDED to come home with us to give me a few lessons on witchcraft, but as soon as we entered through the door she proceeded to update our grandmother on what had happened earlier that day.

"You're lucky that he didn't take you seriously," Rose said.

"I guess I am," I agreed not really in the mood for another lengthy discussion on the matter.

"Did you happen to tell the detective where your spell led you?" Rose asked, with quite an inquisitive look in her ghostly eyes.

"No," I said. "I don't think throwing Hunter under the bus would have helped prove my case. It would only have made Jack more suspicious."

"Jack?" Scott asked as he headed for the paperback

he left in the dining room. I wondered just how many books he was reading at the same time. "I didn't know you two were on a first name basis."

I rolled my eyes. "Don't even go there," I warned him.

Scott lifted his hands in surrender, but he still kept on talking. "First Hunter, now Jack. You're quite popular with the gents in this town, aren't you?"

"Both men you should definitely not get involved with," Rose said as she held her hands on her hips. I wondered how that worked. Did she feel solid to herself?

"Yes, mother," I said as I once again rolled my eyes.

"I'm hungry," Rhi announced and I was glad for a change of topic.

"Me too," I agreed.

After the three of us made some sandwiches in the kitchen, we retired to the living room and ate. Rhi and I were watching a trashy reality show on television while Scott tried to ignore us as he read his book.

"I think I miss food the most," Rose said as she floated back and forth in front of the television. If she wasn't see-through, I would have had a few choice words for her.

"Must suck to be a ghost," Rhi agreed as she made a point of munching down on her sandwich.

I laughed. "This is too weird," I said. In fact, the

whole thing was surreal. Ghosts, magic, murders, it was all a little too much for me.

"You'll get used to it," Rhi said, though I wasn't as confident about that as she was.

After we ate Rhi led me up to the attic for my first official magic lesson. Scott wanted to follow but Rhi stopped him.

"No mundanes allowed," she said and left it at that. Scott looked crestfallen and I sent him an apologetic look. He went back to the living room and resumed reading his book. I felt sorry for him, but all of this was new to me so I deferred to Rhi.

After closing the door behind us, Rose soon joined us in the attic.

I looked around. I paid especial attention to the spellbook on the table.

To be honest, I've never been much of a book person. Give me the movie or TV version any day of the week, but there was something different about *this* book. It was like it was calling to me and every time I saw it I had the incredible urge to touch it. To hold it. To leaf through its many pages.

I reached out to take a hold of it but Rhi gently snapped it away.

"A real witch shouldn't rely on books. She should rely on her own experience."

"I did cast a spell yesterday," I told her.

"That was a spell from a book. It was a recipe you

followed. That magic has its place, but if you want to be a really powerful witch you need to focus on the magic inside you, not outside you."

Rose nodded as she stood back and let Rhi take charge.

"I don't really know if I've ever felt any magic inside me…"

"You have," my grandmother said. "That necklace around your neck kept you protected and brought you back here when you needed to be here the most. Did you not feel its magic pulling you back to Hazelville?"

I took the pendant in my hand and touched it. It was warm to the touch. In fact, I did feel something pulling me back home, but it didn't feel like it was anything magical. It seemed more like it was a financial reason than anything. I didn't voice those thoughts out loud, though.

"I guess, but I can't be sure," I finally said.

"Either way, your first lesson will be to get in touch with that magic that all witches have inside them."

Rhi instructed me to sit down cross-legged on the floor. It took a while for me to find a comfortable position. After I did, I closed my eyes and breathed in deeply.

"Breathe in and out slowly, letting the tension in your body dissipate with each out breath. With each in breath, breathe in relaxation."

I did as I was told and surprisingly I found myself

relaxing into a light trance almost immediately. Before I'd always thought that I was too scatterbrained for meditation, but it seemed that wasn't the case now. Perhaps I just needed the right teacher, or the right incentive. After all, who wouldn't want to meditate if they knew it would lead to magical powers?

"Can you feel something around you?"

I focused on feeling around me and to my surprise I could feel a certain energy emanating all around.

"Yes," I answered. "It's everywhere..."

"Exactly," Rhi agreed. "Now pull some of that energy inside you. Do it however it feels most natural to you."

I focused on letting the energy in through the top of my head. I let it fill my body until it started to overflow. I felt like I could float away.

"Now focus this energy, this power. Collect it in a central location and then guide it toward your hands."

I did as I was told and found it to be incredibly easy. My eyes were still closed, but I had my hands, palm to palm, right in front of me. I let the energy pool between them until it took up a naturally spherical shape.

"Open your eyes."

I did, and when I saw the glowing ball of energy between my palms I gasped in shock. The energy lost form until it disintegrated into thousands of tiny specks that soon dissipated.

"Wow," I said in amazement as I enjoyed the show. "What was that?"

"Magic," Rhi simply said. "Now let's work on keeping it in one place."

The rest of the evening went by quickly, but when I finally saw the time, four hours had passed. I had so much fun I hadn't even noticed.

Rhi showed me how to use the magical energy for a variety of tasks. To create shields, charge objects with certain energies, and even send it on simple tasks.

"Find the cat," I sent a mental picture of the cat to one of the energy balls I created. The ball disappeared through the door.

It took a couple of minutes for us to hear the cat scratching on the attic door. I opened it and the cat ran inside and joined Rose and Rhi.

I pet the cat with a huge smile on my face.

Being a witch was going to be more fun than I thought.

SCOTT DIDN'T LOOK TOO happy when we finally made our way down. I said goodbye to Rhi and I closed the door behind me when she finally drove away.

"Are you still pissed about being excluded?" I asked Scott as I sat next to him on the couch.

Scott didn't say a word, which pretty much answered my question.

"Look, I'm sorry," I said. "But you're not a witch."

"Tell me something I don't know," Scott said sarcastically. He still didn't take his gaze from the paperback in his hand, though I could see that he wasn't actually reading the words in front of him.

The cat joined us by sitting on the table in front of us.

"What's your name, kitty-cat?" I asked the creature as it looked at me judgmentally while licking its paw.

"Familiars are slow to reveal themselves," Rose said when she joined us.

"It's getting crowded here," Scott said as he got up to go. "Good night."

I thought about going after him but decided against it. He needed some time. I knew that we needed to have a talk, but it could wait. Besides, I already had my hands full with this witch stuff.

"What do you mean?" I asked my grandmother once I was sure that Scott was gone.

"This is not a regular cat, Rory," my grandmother said. "This is a magical cat that will prove indispensable to you in the future."

"It doesn't look any different from other cats to me. Besides, I've barely seen it since I arrived. Frankly, I don't think it likes me much."

Rose laughed. "It's not about liking you, it's much deeper than that. The fact that it's already here means that it sensed something in you. It will only be a matter of time now that you've started your training."

I sighed. I didn't know what to say. I reached out and

pet the cat but it batted my hand away and resumed its bathing.

"At least it didn't scratch you," Rose offered but not surprisingly her words didn't make me feel any better.

"I think I need some air," I finally said. "I think I'll go for a drive."

"That's not a good idea," Rose said. "There's a killer on the loose."

"I think I'll be okay," I said as I got up to go.

I picked the keys up and put on my jacket. However, when I tried to open the front door, my grandmother appeared in front of it.

"Rory, I can't let you go out alone at night. Ask Scott if he wants to join you," she said.

"You know I can go right through you, right?"

Rose nodded but didn't move out of the way.

"I need some time alone," I said as I reached through her and opened the door.

I said goodbye and got the hell out of there. The moment I left the house I felt a sense of relief wash over me.

Rose's car was a bug way past its prime, but at least it was something. The gas was half full so I decided not to go too far. To be frank, I wasn't really sure what I was doing. It was past midnight and I should have probably gone to bed and called it a night, but now that I'd felt the magic all around me, I couldn't stand still for some reason.

I drove aimlessly around, almost on autopilot.

I drove in circles for a while until I finally ended up in front of Book & Candle. I parked the car where Rhi usually left hers and got out.

Everything looked fine on the outside, but I couldn't shake the feeling that something was wrong. I peeked in through the new glass window and thought I saw a flash of light in the back.

Maybe it was just my imagination, but I decided to check it out anyway.

The store's keys were on the same keychain as the car's. I decided to use the back door. I did not want to alert anybody by setting off the bell at the front door.

I walked to the back. When I reached the back door I knew someone was there. The door was slightly ajar. There was a small slip of cardboard keeping the door open.

I took in a deep breath and filled myself with the energy around me. I let the energy pool in my hand and solidify.

It took all my concentration to keep it there, but somehow I managed it. I slowly opened the door with my other hand, making sure that I made as little noise as possible.

It was dark and the only source of light was the ball of energy in my left hand.

I heard sounds coming from the top. The attic. Rose's private magic room.

I saw a dark figure on top of the stairs. I could not make out who it was but by the sounds of frustration that I heard I knew that the intruder wasn't having much luck.

A couple of expletives later, I decided it was time to crash the party.

"Who are you?" I asked, my voice maybe a little too loud, a little too confident under the circumstances. But I was a witch, and the magic was inside me. I felt invincible, though I knew that that was probably not the best idea.

The dark figure ran down the stairs and whooshed right past me. I wasn't having none of that.

I sent a mental picture to the energy ball in my hand. It flew up and traveled and went straight for the intruder. It hit the dark figure and threw the figure across the floor.

"Shit," I heard the intruder hiss as he hit the floor hard.

I flipped the light switch in the corner as the figure slowly rose to reveal himself.

It was Hunter.

SEVENTEEN

My cell phone was in my hand as soon as I saw who it was.

"Stay where you are," I warned him.

Hunter dusted himself off and gave me his best smile. I rolled my eyes. I had no time for silly flirtations under such serious circumstances.

"I see you've learned a trick or two," he said. "I'm impressed."

"I don't care what you think," I said. "Stay where you are and stay there until the cops get here."

"That's not such a hot idea," Hunter said. That smile again.

"And why not?"

"What would you tell them?"

"I'd tell them the truth. That you broke into my store. What else do you think they need to know?"

"Maybe they'd like to know how exactly you managed to find me here, and more interestingly, how you managed to subdue me." He took another step toward me and I took one back. I had no physical weapon and my body was too full of adrenaline to connect to the magical energy around me.

"Stay where you are," I warned him. "Or I'm definitely calling the police."

Hunter lifted his hands up in mock surrender. "No need to do something we'll both regret."

"Why are you here? And why did you try to break into the attic room?"

"I just came to collect what's rightfully mine," Hunter said.

His words rang true, but I had no idea why. Some sort of magical intuition? Or maybe it was a spell of Hunter's that was manipulating my thought processes. If I was smarter, I would have just called the cops and let them deal with it.

"I'll tell you everything," Hunter said, growing restless. "Let's go for a drink or something."

"I'm not going anywhere with you."

"C'mon, I don't bite," Hunter urged me and I relaxed a little. There was something about him that was so cool and collected that it made me feel the same.

He ran his hands through his shoulder length hair that was longer than mine. He smiled that devilish smile again.

"I'm not the bad guy here," he said.

"Then who is?"

"I'll tell you once you join me for drinks."

"Fine," I was surprised by the word coming out of my mouth. There was something definitely going on between us, and I wasn't so sure it was just a matter of infatuation on my part.

"I'll follow you there," I said as I motioned for him to get out of the shop.

I checked the attic door, but it looked undisturbed. Either I came just in time, or the wards there did their job.

I locked the door behind me as I watched in amazement as Hunter stood by empty space.

"Where's your bike?"

He smiled and uttered some unintelligible words as he ran his hands through empty air. The motorcycle became visible almost instantly. It was always there, I somehow knew, I just wasn't able to register it. Now I could.

I was impressed, but thankfully I refrained from saying so. I got in the bug and followed Hunter to a nearby bar. The same one we'd been in before.

I was surprised how busy it was now. Was this the hour that professional alcoholics decided to come out in droves?

As soon as we got our drinks (a rum and coke for me

and a scotch on the rocks for Hunter) I went right to business.

"Convince me why I shouldn't call the cops," I said and took a gulp of my drink.

Hunter eyed me as he took a sip of his own. It seemed that he wasn't in the mood to talk.

"It's a long story," he finally said as I rolled my eyes in response.

"I've got time."

"It's a family feud between your grandmother and my parents."

"Tell me something I don't know. She told me all about it. How her store was more successful than your parents' and you had to move out of town because of it."

A sad smile lingered on Hunter's face. "That's not how I remember it."

His reluctance to spill any details had me more than intrigued. I finished my rum and coke out of frustration but refused another. After all, I had to drive myself home.

"I'm listening," I finally said, waiting for him to continue.

"The way my father told it, your grandmother stole a good luck artifact that's been in my family for generations. That's why her store did so much better than theirs."

Thinking of my sweet dead grandmother, I could not

fathom her doing such a thing. Either Hunter was mistaken or he was outright lying.

"If that's true, which I don't believe it is, why didn't your parents just get it back, or steal it back in this case?"

"That's what I was trying to do today. Back in the day, your grandmother was the most powerful witch in town. When I heard she died, I thought..."

"You could just swoop in and steal from my family?"

"I like to think of it as taking back, rather than stealing."

"Why didn't you just ask me? Maybe I would have..."

"Showed me the door?"

"I wouldn't have done that. But catching you stealing, well, it doesn't make me want to listen to anything you have to say."

"I'm sorry," Hunter said. He looked beaten down and fairly miserable. "I shouldn't have done that."

"Maybe I can consult with my cousin. Maybe there's a way for you to get that artifact back without breaking into my store again."

"Maybe," Hunter said but sounded doubtful.

There was nothing left to be said. Hunter apologized as he walked me out. I told him to sit tight while I did my own research into the matter.

"HE'S A LIAR. He comes from a family of liars, and it

wouldn't surprise me if he was a murderer as well," Rhi said when I told her about Hunter's request. (I refrained from mentioning of catching him in the act of trying to steal the object from the store. I knew that she would call the police.)

"I concur. The Crowleys are not to be trusted," my grandmother chimed in.

As usual, Scott had his head in a book.

We were in Book & Candle and it seemed like my innocent question had made quite an impact on the Wiltz women.

I myself had no idea what the big deal was. The Crowleys vs the Wiltzs seemed like a feud made in hell, and I wasn't even sure why. If Hunter was to be trusted, it was because my grandmother was a thief, but of course, I couldn't come right out and say it.

"So this good luck artifact or object or whatever it is has been in our family since when?"

"A long, long time," Rose said.

"For as long as I remember," Rhi agreed.

It was settled then. Either my grandmother and cousin were lying for some reason, or Hunter was mistaken.

I decided to drop the subject for the foreseeable future.

"Any leads on the car wreck case?" Rose finally asked.

The car wreck case? "The only lead we had was

Hunter, and since it's our word against his, and we have no actual physical proof, we're at a standstill."

"Maybe if you were actually looking for clues instead of listening to his lies, we wouldn't be," Rhi said off-handedly. I was so shocked by her words that I didn't know how to respond.

"Rory is not a detective or a PI," Scott chimed in. "Why do you guys act like it's her responsibility to solve murders in this town? She's doing the best she can under the circumstances."

I was glad that Scott wasn't mad enough at me to completely ignore while I was being ganged up on. I mouthed a thank you in his direction as Rose and Rhi seemed to be at a loss for words.

"Well, of course she's not, but..." Rose started to say.

"But you promised to try," Rhi added.

"Yeah, but I think you guys expect too much of me. I think we should let the police handle this one. I mean, where should I go from here?"

Scott put his book down again. "I might have an idea," he said, suddenly coming to life.

"What is it?" I was desperate for any direction.

"If we can't investigate the culprit, let's focus in on the victims. Maybe there'll be a clue as to who wanted them dead."

"That's a great idea," I told Scott. "Rhi, you'll be okay here by yourself?"

Rhi nodded but looked uncertain. "Didn't you

already talk to the ghosts of the two boys? That didn't get you very far."

"Yes, but I was going about it the wrong way. I should not focus on their deaths, I should focus on their lives."

"Good luck," Rose said as we exited the store. She didn't look too certain about our prospects, but to tell the truth, I was just glad to get out of there.

"IT'S A LOT OF PRESSURE. It's weird. Especially once you think about the stuff Hunter said," Scott was saying as I focused on driving.

"Yeah, I mean I didn't know this inheritance was going to come with this much trouble."

"Amen to that," Scott said and laughed. "Oh, there's the junkyard."

"Do you really think this is the best idea?" I asked as I parked the car in what I hoped would be an inconspicuous spot. It was midday and I felt a lot more exposed than when we went there at night.

"It's open now," Scott said. "We can just walk in, we don't have to break in, so technically we're not breaking any laws right now."

He had a point there. I just hoped that Detective Morgan would keep his distance.

We walked right in like it was nothing and no one said a word. We looked around awhile but couldn't find the car.

"Do you think he had it moved after the incident?" I asked Scott and he nodded.

"Probably. Maybe they put it in a garage or something."

I looked around and couldn't even spot the two victims.

"Any ideas?"

"Do you remember their names?" Scott said.

"Yeah, I think so."

"Let's find a phone book or directory and go from there."

I DROVE while Scott looked through the phone book.

"Are you sure we're going the right way?" I asked as we kept driving into a further and further isolated area. It looked like we were in a park. There were a few trailers scattered around.

"I'm pretty sure they live in a trailer park. Or lived, should I say," Scott said as he flipped back and forth through the phone book in his hands

I kept on driving until the road became a dirt road and then until there was no road at all. When I saw a bunch of cars parked in the distance I decided to join them.

"This looks like it," Scott said as we got out of the car.

"Are you being serious right now?"

"Where else did you expect those juveniles to live?"

"That makes sense I guess."

"I told you I knew what I was talking about."

Scott and I walked carefully around. There were a few locals who gave us dirty looks, but thankfully no one took out their gun and started shooting at us. I myself wasn't sure what to expect. I was never in this part of town when I lived here, then when I moved to New York I didn't have a lot of opportunities to visit a trailer park.

"What's the address again?" I asked Scott.

"Peaches and Pearl 42?"

"Is that a question?"

"Sorry, it just sounds weird."

We spent the next ten minutes in silence as we walked around the trailer park, trying to locate the right address. Most of the trailers did not have a name, then those that did, did not sound even close to what we were looking for.

"There it is!" Scott said as he pointed out a blue trailer in the distance, a little farther than all the other ones.

"What makes you think that's the right trailer?"

"The little sign right there, it says Peaches and Pearl Hairdresser."

"Oh," I said. "Do you think I should get my hair done?"

"Very funny, Rory."

"I try my best."

The time for jokes was over. We were approaching the trailer and I knew this was a serious matter.

"Do we even know what we're going to say to them?"

"I didn't really think about it," I said. "Maybe we could say we were friends of theirs. Is this Nathan or Boyd's house?"

"Nathan," he said. "Boyd should be a couple of trailers over."

"How lovely," I said. "No wonder they turned to crime. This place has already bored me half to death and I haven't even been here fifteen minutes. Imagine growing up here."

"Amen to that," Scott said. Then he made a face. "Is that a bad thing to say to a witch?"

"You know what, I don't really know. But I don't really mind."

"Here it goes," Scott said as we approached the trailer.

"Should I pretend that I'm here for a hair appointment?"

Scott looked around dubiously. There were a few women in the distance which huge puffy hair that looked out of date a couple of decades at least. "I don't think that's such a good idea..."

"I get your point."

I knocked on the door and waited for someone to answer.

THE WOMAN who opened the door did not look like the kind of hairdresser I would have liked to go to. Her hair was a mess. She had bags under her eyes and her makeup was all wrong. I knew that she had just lost her son, but somehow I suspected that this wasn't much different from the look she sported before the tragic events that just happened.

"What the hell do you want?" The woman asked, obviously annoyed by our presence. I wondered if her name was Peaches or Pearl. I'd bet my hair on Pearl.

I took a deep breath. "Hi, I just wanted to give you my condolences on the loss of your son."

"Who the hell are you? Are you one of those religious nuts? Jehovah's witnesses? I have no time for this crap."

"No, no, I was a friend of your son's."

"Oh, is that it, you've come here for your drugs? You sure look like a druggie."

"Oh, you're one to judge," I regretted the words as soon as they left my mouth. The woman had just lost her son, and here I was having a verbal spat with her.

"We're not here for drugs, we're just here to give our condolences on your loss," Scott said carefully. I was surprised how calm he was.

"Well? Is there anything else?"

"Actually, there is," Scott said.

I had no idea what Scott was talking about. What was his plan?

"I was actually here to see if you had a book of mine that your son borrowed," Scott said. As soon as I heard the words, I knew we were in trouble.

The woman laughed and then she slammed the door in our faces.

"Excellent work, Sherlock," I said as we walked in the direction of the other trailer.

"It was the best I could have come up with at that exact moment," Scott said. "I do admit it wasn't one of my best moments."

"You think so?"

We walked over to the next trailer. "What's the name of this one?"

"Shells and Mermaids."

"Are these boats or trailers?"

"Don't look at me," Scott said defensively. "I didn't name them."

I approached the next trailer with some hesitation. This was where Boyd had lived. I hoped his family was friendlier than Nathan's.

The man who opened the door after we knocked looked like a cliché of trailer park trash. He had a white barely there T-shirt, a huge beer gut, and a balding head.

Oh, and his attitude wasn't much better than Nathan's mother's.

"What the hell do you want?"

I did the talking this time. "Hi, I was dating your son."

The man looked incredulous but then his features softened when he looked me up and down. I wasn't sure if that was a good thing or a bad thing.

"And who is this?"

"Oh, this is my brother Scott. I'm Rory by the way."

I extended my hand and immediately regretted it, but now that it was out here I could not take it back. The man shook my hand longer than was necessary. It was sweaty and clammy all at once, and it took all my strength not to cringe right in front of him.

The man smiled. "Do come in," he said.

I wasn't so sure this was a good idea now. Before, our goal was to get in and talk to the families of the two boys, but now that I saw exactly what that entailed, I was hesitant. Thankfully, I had Scott with me. Hopefully that would stop the man from making any moves.

The trailer was as expected. Too small, too cluttered, and empty beer bottles everywhere.

We sat on a small couch and refused offers of drink. The man of the house took a beer for himself and joined us.

"Funny, my boy Boyd never said anything about you."

"Oh we've been dating for the last couple of months,

nothing serious, but I was still devastated when I heard about the accident."

"That was no accident," the man said and cringed. "At least not according to what that fancy detective told me."

"Oh, what exactly did he say?"

Boyd's father blabbered on about the same information we already knew while I tried to come up with an excuse to get into Boyd's room. I looked around the trailer and wondered where exactly that would be.

"May I see Boyd's room?"

"Why?"

"Closure, I guess," I said, trying to sound as sad and sincere as possible. "I just need something to remember him by."

"I guess that won't be a problem," he said. "But as you well know, Boyd did not spend a lot of time here. His favorite place to hang out was the lake in the back of the woods. He always hung out with that kid Nathan. You can imagine the worries I had, but thankfully you have just proved that my boy was not a sissy, but a real man." The man said as he looked me up and down, a strange kind of hunger in his eyes. I fought the urge to retch right there and then.

I looked over at Scott; he did not look much better. I could see that he wanted to say something to the man and that he was holding back. That was smart, we did not need to antagonize this man since he was being so helpful.

Boyd's room was just a bed, a chair and some dirty magazines on the floor. There was a bunch of dirty clothes on the floor too. It was obvious that Boyd only used this room for sleeping and not much else.

"Thank you so much for your time," I said after we looked through the room, and I couldn't find anything that anyone would want to take with them as remembrance of someone who died too young.

"You're welcome to come back anytime," Boyd's father said as he wished us a good day.

"Now that's how it's done," I said to Scott as we walked down toward the woods in the distance.

"Please, that was the easiest thing in the world."

"Then why didn't you try it with Nathan's mother?"

"Eww," Scott said and made a face.

We walked our way through the woods, and thankfully did not run into any of the locals. Once we saw the lake in the distance, we both sighed in relief. Boyd's father was telling the truth. He was not going to come out here and hunt us down like we had feared. Or at least like *I* had feared.

"Do you see what I see?" Scott asked me as he pointed in the direction of two silhouettes standing by the lake.

"It's Boyd and Nathan, isn't it?"

EIGHTEEN

We approached the two figures carefully, just in case they turned out to be living people. But as we approached, I noticed that we could see through the silhouettes.

"Hello there," I said as we walked up behind them.

The two ghosts turned around and the scowls on their faces were as unpleasant as ever. They became even more unpleasant once they recognized who we were.

"You two again?" Nathan said.

Boyd and Nathan looked like they were ready for a fight. But they already knew they could not take us on, so I don't know what they were trying to prove.

"I just had a little chat with your father, Boyd," I said. The look on Boyd's face was priceless.

"You shouldn't have done that," he said as he approached me.

Of course, I did not move out of the way. There was nothing Boyd could do to me. He was a ghost.

"We're just here to ask you guys a couple of questions," I said. "After that, you can do whatever you want to do."

"And why should we help you?" Nathan asked. It was clear that Nathan was the alpha in this relationship. Boyd seemed meeker somehow, more like a follower than a leader.

"If you help us, you will only be helping yourselves. Scott and I are trying to solve your murders, remember?"

"We don't need your help," Nathan said.

"That's right," Boyd agreed.

The two ghosts seemed awfully confident for someone recently dead.

"Just tell us what you remember, anything would be helpful," Scott said, looking like he wanted to be anywhere but there.

"We already told you, we don't remember who killed us," Nathan said.

"So, this is your favorite place to hang out?" I asked the two boys.

My question took them by surprise. That was exactly my intention. I needed them to relax so that we could finally get some useful info out of them. The two boys didn't say anything. They seemed at a loss for words.

"What happened to your car?" Scott asked.

"They took it away, and we got bored. Then somehow we found ourselves here by the lake." Boyd said, and quickly retreated into the background once Nathan gave him an angry look.

"You can't go anywhere you want?" I asked.

"No, we can't. I thought being a ghost would be much more fun."

"I bet you did," I said and smiled. My implication was clear. They could've been spying on cheerleaders right now, but here they were standing by a depressing looking lake.

"What would you say if I said I was willing to do you a favor?" I asked.

"Yeah, any unfinished business you guys have, we can help you out with."

"Wow, that's really…"

"Shut up, Boyd," Nathan said.

"What? It's not like they're coming back."

"It's not like who's coming back?" Scott asked, suddenly intrigued by the two youths.

"None of your business," Nathan said.

"We can't help you if you don't tell us the truth. Why does it matter anyway? You're already dead, what else do you have to lose?"

Nathan and Boyd retreated further back from us.

Apparently, they did not like being questioned about anything surrounding the cause of their deaths. I had a feeling that they knew much more than they were letting on.

"Did someone hire you guys to throw that rock through my window? Was it Hunter Crowley?"

"Who?" Boyd asked, before realizing that he should have kept his mouth shut.

But this was a good thing. They did not know who Hunter was. That meant that Hunter was probably not involved in their deaths.

"Come on," Nathan said to Boyd as he took his hand. The two juveniles disappeared into thin air.

OUR LITTLE VISIT to the trailer park left us with more questions than answers. It was obvious that the two youths were hiding something, but it was also obvious that they were not willing to talk to us about any of it. Well, at least Nathan did not. Boyd was the weaker link. But we did not have the option of talking to him alone. Nathan was always there.

I suddenly had an idea, and I turned the car around abruptly.

"Are you trying to kill us?" Scott asked angrily.

"Sorry, I just remembered seeing something peculiar. We're going back to the trailer park," I said.

I drove us back to where we came from. Now, I did

not expect to see the ghosts again. They obviously moved back to the location of their vehicle or some other spot the ghosts liked when they were still alive.

No, there was just something weird I noticed by Nathan's trailer.

I got out of the car with purpose. I walked over to where the sign for Peaches and Pearl Hairdresser was. There was a small baggie hanging from the sign and as soon as I touched it I felt a spark and immediately took my hand back.

"What was that?" Scott asked me.

"Magic," I said confidently.

The door of the trailer flung open and Nathan's mother looked furious.

"I thought I told you two to get the hell off my property?" She yelled as she chased after us with a broom. Scott and I ran back to the car as fast as we could. Nathan's mother got a couple of hits at my car, but thankfully it was already beat up so it didn't make much difference.

"What the hell was all that about?"

"We just got our first clue, Scott."

"THAT CERTAINLY IS WEIRD," Rhi said.

"Is it possible that they bought that charm bag or whatever you said it was, here?" I asked.

"Anything is possible, but I highly doubt it. She

probably got it from a local witch around where she lives."

"I guess that makes sense," I said, defeated.

It seemed that our little clue was another dead end. When I saw that magical bag I thought for sure it meant that a witch was involved in the deaths of Nathan and Boyd. But now I wasn't so sure. Maybe Nathan's mother was just a fan of magical charms and such and was just superstitious and had no idea that the bag she had there actually had real magical properties. But what if his mother was a witch too?

I asked Rhi about it but she seemed pretty sure that that wasn't the case.

"How can you be so sure?"

"Did you feel anything when you were talking to her?"

"Besides the animosity?"

"Yes, besides that."

"No, I didn't sense anything special about her."

"Then there's your answer. She's probably just a fan, a mundane who goes around magic shops and buys trinkets here and there, hoping that her luck would improve. But since she's still living in a trailer park, I doubt it works too well for her."

I found Rhi to be awfully judgmental, but I couldn't disagree with her.

The rest of the day passed in relative boredom. I

myself was not exactly sure what was going on. It seemed our trip to the trailer park was a bust.

"What do you think about the ghosts of Nathan and Boyd?"

"What about them?" Rhi asked as she surfed the net on her laptop. Not surprisingly there were no customers inside. Maybe she was fulfilling online orders. I certainly hoped so for our sake.

"Well, they seemed like they knew something. And then they just disappeared."

Before Rhi had a chance to answer, and probably dismiss my suspicions, the bell chimed and both of us looked at the entrance.

It was just Bobby, the delivery guy. He was delivering a box of something to the store.

Rhi's face lit up as soon as she saw him. Looking at Bobby, he didn't look like much. He was a little over-weight, his hairline was receding, but I guess he had a good-natured quality about him that Rhi liked.

"Hi Rhi, hi Rory. I just got your latest shipment of incense."

"Thanks," Rhi said and took out a pen to sign the slip he gave her.

I took the box to the back, giving them privacy to catch up or talk or whatever.

I found Scott sitting there in the back reading another paperback. This seemed like the perfect opportunity to talk to him about what exactly he was doing in Hazelville.

"So, are you still planning on going back to New York?"

"I'm not sure," Scott said, as he put his book down. "There's so much going on here with you, I'm kind of afraid to leave you alone. There's a murderer on the loose, maybe more than one. What kind of a friend would I be if I left you to fend for yourself out here?"

"I guess you have a point there."

"I have been looking into any available jobs around here. There might be a reporter position at the local newspaper."

"That sounds perfect for you, but you know you can always work for me."

"Really? Do you really think that's a good idea?"

"Why not?" I asked, genuinely curious. It seemed like the perfect fit. Scott was my best friend and I just inherited a shop, and half of it was made out of books. Sure, they were of the occult variety, but they were still books. If Scott couldn't find a job anywhere else, he could always come and work for me. And if what Rhi had said about the online sales was true, I would actually have money to pay him.

"If you had inherited Booked for Murder, maybe I'd see your point. But working here...I don't think I'd be too comfortable."

"Fair enough," I said.

I heard the bell chime again and either we had someone else coming in, or more believably Bobby was done and leaving. I decided to join Rhi in the front and actually saw a new face by the counter. I did not recognize this fellow, though he looked somehow familiar. It was a weird feeling, and when I came closer, I could see that his energy signature was not of a mere mundane. He was magical, just like me and Rhi.

"How can we help you?" I asked as I joined Rhi behind the counter. Rhi seemed at a loss for words.

"I'm just looking around, but thanks." The fellow said, and turned around to look at the various crystals, candles and incenses in one corner of the store.

Rhi gave me a strange look and I wondered what she was trying to say.

"Do you know who he is?" I whispered to her when I was sure the strange customer was out of earshot.

"Well, I'll be on my way," Bobby said.

Both Rhi and I said our quick goodbyes, but all our attention was on the new arrival.

I observed the stranger closely, and he seemed more interested in his surroundings than the products that we were selling. He was strange, but what could I do? I couldn't come right out and ask what he wanted.

"Lovely place you've got here," the stranger said as he approached the counter without anything in his hands. "I'll probably be back later, right now I have to be somewhere."

"Have a nice day," I said to the stranger. Just as he was about to open the door he turned around and smiled. He had piercing green eyes and short dark hair. He definitely reminded me of someone, I just couldn't place who.

"That was weird," I said to Rhi.

She nodded. "He's definitely a witch."

For some unknown reason, a shiver went up my spine. While I couldn't believe Hunter was responsible for my grandmother's death, or the deaths of the two teenagers, I could definitely believe this guy was capable. There was just something about the look in his eyes. It was almost as if there was nothing behind them.

"What do you think he really wanted?" I asked Rhi.

"Beats me," she said. "But we definitely need to be vigilant. He seemed like he was more interested in the store than anything we were selling. He might be back."

"I'd bet my life on it." As soon as those words left my mouth, I realized how ominous they actually sounded.

"So what about Bobby?" I asked her in an effort to change the subject.

"What about him?" Rhi seemed oblivious to the insinuation in my question.

"He seems to really like you, is all."

"Really?" Rhi asked, a look of bewilderment in her eyes. It seemed she was completely oblivious to his feelings for her.

"It's pretty obvious that he likes you. I guess he just doesn't have the nerve to ask you out."

Rhi smiled as she thought about what I was saying. "He's nice, but I can't really think of him as anything else than just a friend."

That made sense, so I decided not to push the issue.

The rest of the day at the store was pretty slow and no other customers made an appearance. Just before we closed up I asked Rhi to help me reinforce the wards around the shop.

"Good idea," she said, suddenly coming back to life.

Rhi walked me through the procedure then we did it together after closing up shop as Scott watched on from the corner of the street. We circled the shop and visualized a huge barrier manifesting around it. After we were done Rhi made me repeat some gibberish words to seal the spell so to speak, and when she beckoned me to touch the barrier, which was invisible of course, I felt a pushback.

"It worked!" I said excitedly.

"Of course it did," Rhi said as if this was the most natural thing in the world. I guess in a way it was, for us anyway.

We said our goodbyes at the cars. Rhi did not have to drive us anymore since I had Rose's bug. Rose did not make an appearance at the store today, and I wondered if it was because she sensed another witch was nearby.

I'd have to ask her about it later, and maybe about that magical baggie that I found in the trailer park.

"Oh, do you want to go out to dinner or lunch with me and Scott?" I asked Rhi when I remembered we had planned to go out.

"Maybe another time, I'm really tired now."

Scott and I watched as Rhi drove away.

"So where exactly are we going?" Scott asked as he put the paperback he was reading at the backseat of the car.

"We'll drive around and see if anything catches our fancy, okay?"

Scott nodded.

NINETEEN

I CHOSE A LOCAL DINER THAT WAS PRETTY CLOSE TO the shop.

"Well isn't this quaint?" Scott said as he looked around the small diner. We were sitting in a booth, and it was surprisingly clean even though the leather seats, or faux leather seats, looked like they needed to be replaced soon.

"It just called to me for some reason," I said.

The waitress looked worn out but friendly. We both ordered grilled cheese sandwiches with a side of fries. As we waited for our food I got to thinking about the two dead juveniles. Maybe the waitress knew them?

Once our food arrived I decided to ask her.

"They've been here a few times, but other than that I didn't know them well. It's a shame about what happened to them."

"Well, that's a dead end," I said to Scott. My grilled cheese sandwich was surprisingly delicious. And the fries were good too. I made a mental note that Shay's Diner was a good place to eat.

"You tried," Scott said. Scott seemed more interested in the food on his plate than the case we were working on. It felt strange to think of it as a case, but wasn't that exactly what it was? It seemed to fall on our shoulders to solve this little mystery. The good detective didn't seem to be getting any closer to figuring out who did it.

Just as I finished my meal and took a sip of my drink I felt a strange sensation come over me. I froze in place as a vision entered my mind. Someone had broken into or rather through the wards me and Rhi had set up earlier. I guess this was some kind of a magical warning.

"What is it? You look like you've seen a ghost," Scott said as he put the remainder of his grilled cheese sandwich down.

"Someone has just broken into the shop."

We drove back as quickly as possible.

"We should call the cops," Scott kept repeating as I drove on ahead.

"What if Rhi came back for something? Maybe that's why the wards set off a warning?" Even as I said the words I knew they didn't make much sense.

Once we were at the shop, I saw an unfamiliar car. It was beat up and it looked like it was on its last legs. I breathed a sigh of relief. It wasn't Hunter again.

"Call the cops," I said to Scott and he did.

I waited with Scott in the car until the cops arrived. The strange car was still outside and I did not want to alert whoever was inside that we knew they were there. I kept my lights off and Scott and I kept our heads low.

Occasionally flashes of light could be seen in the dark shop. Someone was definitely looking for something.

A familiar car joined us in the parking lot. It was Detective Jack Morgan. While I wasn't his biggest fan, after all he did accuse me of murder, I was kind of glad to see a familiar face. I didn't know if I had the nerve to deal with anybody new tonight.

Jack tapped on our window and we got up. I slid the window down and told him everything Scott had told the dispatcher. There was a strange car, and someone had just broken into my shop.

"It's lucky that you caught them in the act," the detective said as he turned to go. Was he suspicious of me? Even if he was, I had no time to think about that.

Scott and I watched from the distance as the detective entered the dark shop. I instinctively sent out a prayer of protection for the detective. I did not want him to get hurt on my count. It was just a shop after all, and not worth anybody's life.

Then a loud noise made me jump out of my skin. I was out of the car in mere seconds, and Scott was right on my tail. A gun had just gone off, and instead of cowering in the car, I ran to see what had happened.

I slowly made my way into the darkened shop and saw a dark figure pointing a gun at the detective. Jack, for his part, was pointing a gun right back at the assailant. Once the dark figure saw me at the back entrance he proceeded to point the gun at me.

"You!" The figure said, his voice familiar. "Give me what I came for and no one has to get hurt."

"Put the gun down," Jack said to the assailant. "I don't want to shoot, but I will if I have to."

A chill went through me because I knew that the words Jack had spoken were true. He had experience using a gun, and I wouldn't have been surprised if he had actually had to kill someone before. In the line of duty, of course.

"I'm not the bad guy here, she is! Her family is the one who stole from mine!"

First Hunter, now this guy? How many people did my grandmother presumably steal from?

I breathed in slowly, relaxing myself. It was hard under the circumstances, but I did my best. I drew up the magical energy inside me and before I had a chance to will it into a ball inside my hand behind my back, the deranged figure wielding a gun put all his attention on me again.

"Don't even think about it," he hissed. "Bullets are faster than spells."

I could imagine the bewildered look on Jack's face, but thankfully all I could see now was the back of his head.

"Drop the gun, or I *will* shoot you," Jack said with authority in his voice.

The dark figure's hand quivered noticeably. I sent the little energy I had raised on a mission to burn the perpetrator's hand. I watched as the ball of energy reached him. His hand lit up, and he dropped the gun almost immediately.

"God dammit," he said as he fell to the ground.

Jack had him in handcuffs in a matter of seconds. I watched as he hauled him out of the store roughly and to the back of his car. In the light of the night lamps, I realized I recognized the crazed gunman. It was the guy who came to the shop earlier that day.

"Do you know this guy?" Jack asked me.

"No, but he did come to my shop today," I said honestly. I was surprised myself that I wasn't lying to him. It seemed I had been doing a lot of that lately.

"Well, just follow me to the station. I need you guys to make a statement."

We did just that.

"Things are getting interesting," Scott said as we followed the detective to the station.

"What do you mean?"

"It seems that everyone's looking for a particular object in your grandmother's shop. Before, we had no idea why anybody wanted to kill her, but now we have a motive. And that brings us one step closer to the killer."

I couldn't argue with that logic. Scott knew more about this stuff than I did, so I was glad he was here by my side.

Jack left us in his office to fill out some paperwork while he took the perpetrator to one of the interrogation rooms.

We waited for the longest time. We watched as he hauled the suspect to the back of the building. Presumably to lock him up in a jail cell.

"You get one phone call," I heard him say to the assailant.

"Who is he?" I asked Jack when he returned to take our paperwork.

"He wouldn't tell me his name. I took his fingerprints so we should know pretty soon."

"Did he say what he wanted from my shop?"

"No, he wasn't very talkative," Jack said as he rearranged the files on his desk. "Do you have any ideas what he wanted in your shop?"

"No, I can't think of anything…" Here I was again lying to the detective.

"Are you sure?" Jack asked both Scott and me. He gave us the sort of look that told us that he knew that we knew more than we were telling and that the ball was in our court.

"If we think of anything, you'll be the first person we'll come to," Scott said.

"What are you doing here?" Jack asked someone behind us. I turned around to see who it was. It was Hunter, and he did not look happy.

"I'm here to talk to my brother," Hunter said.

"So the mysterious assailant is your brother?" Jack asked Hunter.

"Yes, you have my brother Carver in custody. Do I have to pay some kind of bail or...?"

"The bail hasn't been set, but you can certainly have a talk with him. Please tell him to cooperate, or it won't look good for him."

"And why is that?"

"He fired a weapon and pointed a weapon at an officer as well as civilians. He's not getting off easy."

"God dammit," Hunter said. This was the first time I had actually seen him so outwardly emotional and angry. It was quite interesting to see.

"I'll take you back to him, but you only have a short time to talk."

"I understand," Hunter said.

Scott and I looked at each other in shock. It seemed Carver Crowley, Hunter's brother, had broken into my shop.

We waited for him to return, and when he did, he

did not look happy to see us. We said our goodbyes to Jack and he promised to keep us up to date on what was happening.

"Do you have anything to tell me?" I asked Hunter as we walked out of the police station.

"Not really," he said and got on his bike.

"Your brother just tried to kill me for one thing, I think you owe me an explanation. Not to mention that you tried to steal the same thing he did."

"I already told you what happened. You decided not to believe me, but it's the truth. Your grandmother stole my family's artifact. It had been in our family for many generations. As you can see, some members of my family did not take it well. Carver is one of them. My parents themselves aren't doing too well either. Ever since that object has left our family, it's been one bad thing after another. I don't blame Carver for what he tried to do, I just don't like the way he went about it. I'm sorry he pointed a gun at you, but I assure you he did not intend to hurt anyone. He just wanted what was ours."

And with that Hunter drove away.

"Hunter tried to break into the shop, too?" Scott asked me. I realized then and there that I had not told him about what happened.

To say that there was a shouting match in the car on our way home would be an understatement.

"Why didn't you tell me?"

"You were acting all weird and jealous and I just didn't have time for it. Plus, I talked to Hunter about it, and I didn't think it would be a good idea to tell Rhi or my grandmother that I caught him in the act."

"I guess that makes sense, but I still don't understand why you didn't talk to me."

"What happened?" Rose asked as soon as we entered through the front door.

"Carver Crowley tried to break into the shop." I had no energy to lie and I had no reason to. She needed to know what was going on.

The look on my grandmother's face was one of anger. "That family," she said with obvious disdain in her eyes.

"Hunter told me that you stole the object from his family," I said to Rose. I was surprised at my own abrasiveness, but we needed to talk about this.

"I did no such thing," she said. "I already told you that they were jealous of my success. I would not stoop so low to steal from another witch, and if I did, I assure you that the Witches' Council would have something to say about it."

"The Witches' Council?"

"Oh yes, my dear granddaughter. There is a witch police out there. If I had indeed done something so callous, I'm sure the Crowleys would have reported me and I would have been investigated, don't you think?"

"That makes sense," I said even as I remembered

Hunter's words. My grandmother was more powerful than the Crowleys, and that they feared her in some way.

Looking at my grandmother now I found that hard to believe. She was just an old lady. She looked like she couldn't hurt a fly.

"I'm sorry, it's just all of this is new to me," I said and hoped that would be enough.

TWENTY

The next day, after closing up the shop, Rhi had come to visit. When I told her what had happened last night, she completely lost it. Needless to say, there was a chain reaction and everyone ended up ganging up on me.

Rose, Rhi, and Scott were all talking over each other. Rhi and Rose mostly ranted about the evils of the Crowleys while Scott berated me for entering Book & Candle while it was being robbed.

"Guys, I think I get it," I finally said.

The voices just kept on ranting.

I decided to go up to my room instead. I simply wasn't in the mood for another lecture. As soon as I locked the door behind me, Rose appeared out of nowhere.

I jumped up a little. "You scared me to death!"

"Oh don't be dramatic, Rory. You're very much alive."

"What are you doing here?"

"I'm here to talk some sense into you once and for all. I was willing to stand back with all this Hunter Crowley stuff, but after what happened with his brother, I'm not so sure that's a good idea. You need to know once and for all what really happened."

"You already told me. Your shop was more successful and the Crowleys were jealous and moved away. You don't need to repeat it again."

"That was the nice version. The issues between the Wiltzs and the Crowleys go much deeper than that. It actually started long before even I was born. Our two families were always at odds with each other. It all came to a head in my lifetime, though. Once I opened a more successful shop, something broke in that family. They started to fling curses at us, and I needed to take drastic measures."

There was a look of sadness on Rose's face. I couldn't help but feel enraptured by her tale.

"They didn't just pack up and leave like I told you earlier. I banished them."

"What? Why?"

"I just told you, silly girl. They were going after the family. I couldn't let them hurt you, could I?"

I nodded in understanding. Suddenly Rose and Rhi's irrational hatred of the Crowleys seemed much more rational.

"But Hunter and Carver are now in town..."

"I guess after I died my banishment died with me. Hazelville will not be a very pleasant place for you to live if the Crowleys decide to make it their home again."

"What do you want me to do about it?"

"I think you should recast the spell I did all those years ago."

I was at a loss for words. If I cast that spell, I'd never see Hunter again. I wasn't sure I could do that.

"I know it'll be hard," Rose said, understanding and caring in her gaze.

"That's an understatement."

"But it must be done."

"Maybe once all of this is over. There're too many questions up in the air for me to do something as drastic as that right now."

"I understand," Rose said and smiled. "You'll do the right thing once the time comes."

Rose's words rang through my mind the entire night. I tossed and turned and couldn't sleep a wink. After hours of trying, I got up and walked up to the attic.

I felt safe up there, especially with the spellbook in my lap. I flipped through its pages and watched as the strange symbols turned into words I could read again.

"What should I do?" I asked the book, but nothing happened. No pages turned on their own. I was left to my own devices and I wasn't sure that was such a good thing.

All this witch stuff was new to me.

"You can't sleep either?"

I looked up and saw Scott standing in the doorway. I motioned for him to join me. He sat next to me on the floor and looked at the open book in my lap.

"Gibberish."

I laughed. "Sorry," I said as I closed the book. I didn't want him to start feeling jealous or anything of the sort. There wasn't much to be jealous of right now anyway. My life was no fairy tale, and Scott knew that better than anyone.

"What did you and Rose talk about?" He finally asked.

"How'd you know we talked at all?"

"She poofed out of the living room as soon as you went upstairs. It doesn't take a genius to figure it out."

I smiled. That's why I loved Scott. He could always surprise me in the best way possible.

"She told me something I didn't know before about the Crowleys and gave me a lot to think about."

"I don't think you have much to think about. Carver Crowley is bad news."

"I know that," I protested. "It's Hunter I'm not so sure about."

"You really like him, don't you?"

"I don't know. Maybe. But not in the way you may

think." I left it at that and Scott was smart enough to drop the subject for now. Neither one of us was in the mood for a long back and forth.

Scott yawned and I yawned in turn.

"I'm so sleepy," he said.

"Me too, but when I try to fall asleep I just lay there awake. I thought I'd do some reading to help me fall asleep faster."

Scott laughed. "I don't think that book will make you sleep any better. Wanna borrow one of my books?"

"Sure. Give me something on the shorter side."

"I've got *Thirteen Problems* by Agatha Christie. It's a collection of short stories."

"Sounds perfect. And when will I be able to read one of *your* stories?"

Scott looked away. I'd asked the wrong question. Scott's writing, just like my feelings for Hunter, were subjects we weren't supposed to be talking about now.

"I'm sorry," I quickly said.

"No, it's okay. I know I should be writing, it's just that every time I start, something comes up. It's this house too. It's very spooky. I can barely keep my mind on reading much less writing."

I nodded. "I can see how that would be a problem. So much has happened since we arrived here, I wonder what will happen next."

"Don't jinx it, Rory! Maybe nothing will happen."

I tried to entertain the idea, but somehow couldn't. I

wanted to believe that the worse of it was over, but it felt like all of this was just the beginning.

"Get some rest," Scott practically ordered me as he got up to go.

I nodded but all I could think about was having a nice long talk with Carver Crowley.

TWENTY-ONE

"This is highly irregular," Jack said as he closed his office door behind me.

"Tell me something I don't know," I told myself before entering the police station that I would hold back on the sarcasm, but Jack was making it very hard.

"Do you want my help or not?" Jack seemed genuinely angered by my nonchalant demeanor.

I sighed. "Of course. He broke into my shop. He fired a gun, for goodness sake. Is there another reason I need to talk to him?"

"You have a point there," Jack said.

"That's what I've been trying to say all along."

It was Jack's turn to sigh. "Fine, but make it quick. I don't want the sheriff walking in and having a fit."

"Where is this mysterious sheriff anyway? I haven't seen him once since I arrived in town."

"He recently came back from vacation," Jack simply said.

It seemed like a sore subject so I decided to drop it. I was just glad that Jack was letting me speak with Carver at all.

Jack walked me over to the jail cells. The only one there was Carver and he did not look happy to see me.

"What the hell is she doing here?" He spat in Jack's direction.

"Settle down. And behave." Jack turned to me. "Are you sure you want to be here alone with him?"

I looked at the metal bars separating me from Carver.

"I think I'll be fine," I said. "I'll make sure to holler if there's any trouble."

"Holler? Really?" Jack said and smiled despite himself.

"Yes, holler," I said seriously.

"Make it quick," Jack said as he closed the door behind him. Thankfully, there was a little window on the door. I hoped Carver wasn't stupid enough to try anything out of the ordinary.

As soon as Jack left us there alone, the air in the room became difficult to breathe.

I turned around and faced Carver Crowley.

He did not look happy to see me. He could barely look at me, and when he glanced my way, all I could see was the hatred in his eyes.

"I'm not talking to you," he said.

Well, this was going to be more difficult than I thought.

"I just wanted to know why you broke into my shop."

"You know why. Hunter told me he talked to you. He thinks you're different, but you're just like the rest of your family. A group of vipers the lot of you."

"That's not very nice. I've never done anything to you. But you have done something to me. You broke into my shop at the dead of night and practically threatened to kill me."

Carver looked away, whether in anger or shame, I could not really tell.

"You have nothing to say for yourself?"

Carver looked back at me and his eyes were full of hatred. "Your family stole from mine. Your grandmother destroyed my family."

I fought the urge to tell him that wasn't true. I did not know that it wasn't, and I wanted to keep him talking. I might not have believed the words that came out of his mouth but I wanted to keep him talking.

"Is this artifact really that important to you? That you'd be willing to kill someone you don't even know?"

"I wasn't going to kill you. The gun was just to scare you. I know you Wiltz witches are powerful and that my magic would be no match to yours. I needed something to give me an edge in case you interrupted me. And you did. How did you get there so quickly anyway? I watched you guys drive away."

"We went to a diner nearby and the warding spell sent me a psychic warning of sorts that the protections were breached."

"Impressive," Carver whistled. "Especially for a newbie witch."

"Hunter told you about me?"

"He's my brother. He tells me everything."

I was angry that Hunter would talk to Carver about me, but I also understood. If my sister Sam was accused of a crime, I would definitely take her side over anyone else's.

"What else did he tell you?"

Carver looked away. "None of your business." He walked back and sat down on the very uncomfortable looking cot.

"I'm not who you think I am," I said as I turned to go.

"Wait," I heard Carver call after me.

I turned around in surprise.

"What is it?"

"Stay away from my brother."

His words took me by surprise though I couldn't pinpoint why.

"Maybe you should tell Hunter to stay away from me," I said and left without another word.

"That was quick," Jack commented as he put some files he was working on away.

"Yeah, he wasn't very talkative. Do you have any leads on Nathan and Boyd? Do you think he might have been involved in their deaths?"

Jack shook his head. "Not likely. He only arrived to town the other day. The murders happened before that. His brother on the other hand…"

"Do you really think Hunter is involved?"

"I honestly don't know," Jack said. He looked more tired than usual. It was clear that he was working overtime on this particular case.

"I don't really see a motive."

"Look at you talking like a detective," Jack smiled and I smiled in turn.

"Scott's influence. He's the mystery buff."

"I hope you guys have stopped playing amateur sleuths."

"Believe me, we learned our lesson," I lied but Jack didn't seem entirely convinced.

"HUNTER? WHAT ARE YOU DOING HERE?" I asked when I ran into him in front of the police station just as I was about to get into my car.

"I think the better question is what are *you* doing here? I have a brother in a jail cell, what's your excuse?"

I'm not gonna lie, his words cut deeper than I thought they would. After all, I was a victim in all of this. His brother was the maniac.

"Maybe I was talking with Detective Morgan about the charges I'm about to press against your brother," I spat back.

Hunter looked away. He had nothing to say to that.

"Look, I'm sorry about what happened, but it's over and done with. I have to be there for my brother now."

"I understand. I just don't understand how you could be so callous toward me. It's not like I made him break into my shop and shoot up the place."

"Look, I really am sorry that happened, I'm not just saying that. But ever since we moved from Hazelville, things haven't been the same for my family. Carver's been in trouble ever since."

"You seemed to have turned out alright," I said and immediately regretted the words.

Hunter smiled that mischievous smile of his and suddenly I didn't regret a word of what I'd said.

"I've had my moments," he said and made his way into the police station.

I watched as he disappeared into the building and wondered what it was about him that made me trust him beyond all reason.

TWENTY-TWO

"So how was the conversation with Carver?" Scott asked me when I came home. I needed to change before going into the shop.

"Not as enlightening as you would think," I said. "He wasn't very forthcoming. Except for the hatred he felt for my family, and by association, me."

Scott put down the book he was reading.

"That sucks," he said. "I thought for sure he would be confessing to killing your grandmother."

"Where is she by the way?" I looked around but couldn't spot a see-through old lady anywhere.

"Haven't seen her since this morning. Maybe she's over at the shop with Rhi."

"That makes sense," I said as I took off my jacket. "I really thought he would confess."

"Is there some kind of spell that would help?"

I thought about going up to the attic and flipping through the pages of the book but just didn't have the energy. "He's a witch, too, so I don't know how useful that would be."

"I still can't believe that Hunter's brother fired a gun in your shop."

"I can't believe it either. It's been one thing after another since I've arrived, and most of it has involved the Carver family. Maybe Rhi and my grandmother were right all along. Maybe he *is* a bad guy and I'm just refusing to see it?"

Scott nodded. "Maybe. But listen to your gut. You always seemed good at reading people. You're far better at it than me."

I couldn't argue with that. When I lived in New York City for a short while and when I went out for auditions, I could spot a slime ball a mile away. Maybe that was one of the many reasons I never made it in the acting industry...

"My gut tells me that Hunter is a good guy, but I'm not sure if my gut is the only one telling me things."

Scott laughed. "You really like him that much?"

"He's a witch. Maybe that's why I'm so drawn to him."

Scott laughed again. "Yeah, I'm sure that tall, dark and handsome look he's got going has nothing to do with it."

"You know I'm not looking for a relationship," I said

seriously. I had sworn off men for the last couple of years. It was just too much drama.

"I didn't say you had to marry the guy."

"I gotta change. Rhi is alone at the shop and she might need some help. Wanna join me?"

Scott shook his head. "No offense, but that place's boring. I can get a lot more reading done here. Plus, maybe I'll finally get some writing done."

"Fair enough," I said.

I was surprised to find someone waiting for me in front of my bedroom.

"Well hello there kitty," I said to the cat sitting there calmly.

All I got in response was *meow*, which was kind of disappointing. Was a talking cat too much to hope for in a world where magic was real?

I checked its food and water dish but found them full. Apparently, Scott was taking good care of the little bugger.

"HE WASN'T MUCH OF A TALKER," I said as I concluded my recollection about what happened with Craver.

"I don't want to sound like a broken record, but I told you that family was bad news."

I wanted to, but I couldn't really disagree with her.

I looked up at the ceiling where the bullet fired. "At

least it doesn't look like we'll need to do any repairs. It's hardly noticeable."

"Small mercies," Rhi agreed.

We spent the rest of the afternoon looking over the inventory. Most of it went right over my head because I couldn't stop thinking about Nathan and Boyd, Rose, and not to mention Hunter and Carver's attempts to steal from me.

"I've got a few errands to run. Are you sure you'll be okay here by yourself?" Rhi said after we were done.

I looked around the shop and then back at Rhi. "Really?"

"I don't mean with the customers and stuff. I was thinking in light of certain events."

"Well, we reinforced the wards and I have Jack's number on speed dial. I think I'll be okay."

"If you say so. I'll be back as soon as I can."

I waved goodbye to Rhi. It was true: this was the first time I was in the shop by myself when it was actually open. Scott was still moping at home. I hoped he'd get over whatever it was that he was upset about. It wasn't my fault he didn't inherit witch powers.

I hoped that he at least worked on his book. I hadn't seen him writing since we arrived. At least he was reading, so I guess that was something.

I was lost in my own thoughts as I mindlessly surfed the web trying to kill time when a familiar bell chime woke me out of my reverie.

When I looked up I saw that it was only Bobby. He had a box in hand. Rhi hadn't said anything about a delivery. She must have forgotten.

"Hi Bobby," I said, glad for yet another distraction. I had no luck finding anything online about either Carver Crowley or Nathan and Boyd. Or maybe I just didn't know where to look. Rhi was much more computer savvy than me. Even Scott was probably better at it than me. I made a mental note to ask him to help me with my search. Any new info we could get would get us closer to the killers.

"Where's Rhiannon?"

The question took me by surprise. It felt strange to hear my cousin's full name.

"She went out to do some errands. She'll be back soon."

"Oh," was all Bobby said as he approached the counter with the box.

"What did we order this time?" I asked with a smile. I still wasn't used to the fact that I was a shop owner. Yet another thing I needed to add to the list: get better acquainted with how things are run at Book & Candle.

Bobby took out a box cutter and proceeded to open the box, then before he could open it, he looked up. There was a strange look in his eyes that gave me the creeps. He looked like he hadn't gotten enough sleep. He reminded me of a zombie.

"You're a witch, aren't you?"

His question took me by surprise. But since we were standing in the middle of an occult shop that I now owned, it wasn't like I could really deny it.

"I guess," I said noncommittally. I wasn't exactly sure where Bobby was going with this.

Bobby held up the box cutter to the light and smiled a sick smile.

"Thou shall not suffer a witch to live," he said in a tone of voice that I'd never heard him speak in before.

"That was a mistranslation!" I quickly said, but Bobby didn't seem to hear my words, or at least he didn't react to them.

Instead, he lunged at me with the box cutter. I quickly threw the box at him, and was not surprised to find it empty, but it got me enough time to go around the counter. Before I could hightail it for the front door, Bobby was on my heel. He tripped me and I fell to the floor.

"Damn it," I hissed as I felt the blade of the box cutter on my jeans. I hit him in the face as hard as I could as I advanced toward the back of the store.

Just my luck, I found the back door locked. The key was back with the register. My only option was the back of the store and the attic above. Would I be able to unlock the attic door before Bobby caught up to me? That was the life or death question.

I quickly took my phone out and pressed on Jack's name. He picked up almost immediately.

"Bobby the delivery guy is at the store and he's trying to kill me!" I quickly said as soon as I heard Jack's voice.

Before I could hear his reply Bobby appeared at the back of the store.

"You need to die, you need to die," he kept repeating like a crazed man.

We played a game of tag around the tables and all the boxes in the room. Before I found the backroom unnecessarily cluttered, but now I was thankful. If Bobby wanted to get to me he had to risk jumping over a lot of boxes, which would give me more than enough time to hightail it to the front of the shop. Instead, he just chased me around the tables, always making sure not to let me get too close to the exit.

"Why are you doing this? Are you a witch hunter?"

Bobby laughed. "A witch hunter?" He laughed again. I didn't know what was so funny.

I took in a deep breath. I tried to relax and connect to the energy all around me, but was out of luck. I just couldn't focus my mind on anything but surviving Bobby's unexpected assault. I wondered why he had targeted me. I barely knew the man.

"Did you kill my grandmother?" I asked him, trying to distract him from his task of trying to kill me.

Bobby laughed again. Then he suddenly stopped. "You must die," he said calmly.

Just when I had lost all hope and thought that I'd spend the rest of my life trying to outrun a madman, the familiar bell chime announced the arrival of someone to the shop. I just hoped it wasn't a clueless customer.

"Don't make a sound," Bobby warned me as he held out the box cutter across one very cluttered table.

"Or you'll do what, kill me twice?" I screamed my lungs out. "Help! Back here!"

I saw Rhi's familiar face. Before she could say a word, the bell chimed again.

"Over here!" I screamed.

"Help!" Rhi yelled back.

Jack's familiar face came into view, and best of all, he had a gun in his hand.

TWENTY-THREE

"Why did you do it, Bobby? Why?" Rhi wailed at the pudgy man.

"I...don't know..." Bobby said as his eyes flitted from one corner of the room to the other. There was no way out for him now.

I comforted Rhi while Jack pointed a gun in the guilty man's direction. I thought about giving a helping hand, but I didn't think the detective would take any overt displays of magic very well.

"Put the knife down," Jack warned Bobby and Bobby quivered.

"Why did you kill the two youths?" I wanted to know.

Bobby looked confused. "They had to die," was all he said. In fact, he kept repeating the phrase as he waved the knife around.

Inch by inch, step by step, Jack was getting closer to the frantic man. My heart nearly beat out of my chest as I watched in shock as Jack managed to tackle the man to the floor.

I heard a loud grunt and was afraid that Jack had been stabbed, but sighed in relief as Jack cuffed the man with expertise.

"I'll need a statement from all of you, but it can wait," Jack said to me and Rhi. He did not see the shocked look of my grandmother who was standing in the corner.

"I guess you never really know people," Rhi said after Jack drove away with Bobby at the back of his car.

"He seemed so nice," I offered. "I never would have guessed that he would be responsible for three murders. Rose, I'm so sorry I didn't believe you," I added as I looked over at my grandmother's ghostly form.

Rose smiled. "It's alright, child. I find it hard to believe myself. All this time I thought the Crowleys were involved..."

"Me too," Rhi said, an apologetic look on her face. "I'm so sorry I doubted your instincts, Rory."

"That's alright," I said. "There's no way you guys could have known. It doesn't make much sense. Why would Bobby want to kill you and why did he go after the two youths?"

"I think I might have a theory, but I don't think you guys will like it," Rhi said carefully.

"Go on," Rose urged her.

"Well, I know I didn't know him that well, but I felt that he was obsessed with me. Maybe he killed you so I could inherit everything? And then Rory got the shop and the house, and he went after her."

"But why go after the two youths?" I asked.

"Maybe because he saw them as a threat to me? Either way, I'm so sorry all of this happened. If only I'd seen the signs…"

I put my arms around her and held her close. "Don't blame yourself for that psycho's actions. There was no way you could have known."

"I'm a witch, I should have known."

"We all get a little blind with the people we think we know," Rose offered. "I know I convicted the Crowleys just because of our past history. Their attempts to steal from me didn't help matters, though."

I nodded. I knew she was right. Carver Crowley was especially in the wrong and I hoped that Hunter could keep him under control.

"I still don't get one thing, though," I said when I remembered.

"What is it, dear?" Rose asked.

"The spell I did to catch Nathan and Boyd's killer. It led me to Hunter. Why would have that happened if Bobby was the actual guilty party?"

"Good question," Rhi agreed. "I'd like to know myself."

"Well," Rose said carefully, clearly trying to mince her words for my benefit. "I have an idea, but I don't think Rory will like it."

"Just spill it, grandma," Rhi said.

"Maybe Hunter Crowley *was* responsible."

"How? That doesn't make any sense." I'd be the first to admit that I was a little biased. I thought I knew Hunter better than anyone in the room, and he just didn't seem capable of anything like that. Maybe his brother Carver, but not Hunter.

"Well, the spell you cast did lead you to him. While Bobby might have done the deeds himself, that doesn't mean that there wasn't someone behind him pulling the strings."

"Is that even possible?" I asked.

"Oh, yes. It would take a powerful witch, but I'm more than certain it's possible. It's also against the rules set by the Witches' Council, and if they found out, it would not be pretty for your friend."

"Are you suggesting that it's not over? That I have to prove that Hunter was actually the one responsible?"

"I'm still here, aren't I?"

I couldn't argue with that. We had all been going on the assumption that Rose would move on after we found her killer. Bobby was in custody, and grandma was still here. That meant that the real killer hadn't been caught yet.

"I'll get to the bottom of this," I finally said.

"What are you going to do?" Rhi asked, concern clear on her face. "You know, Hunter could be more dangerous than you realize..."

"I know," I said. "I'll be careful."

I FOUND Hunter at the bar area at the inn he was staying.

"Did you hear?" I asked him as I took a seat next to him. He was holding an empty glass.

"Hear what?" Hunter asked, not really seeming in a talkative mood. It was understandable with all the stuff with his brother.

"Bobby has just been arrested for all three murders. He confessed to killing my grandmother."

"That's good, I guess," Hunter said, though he didn't seem too convinced by what I was saying.

"It is. Now my grandmother can finally move on," I said and realized my mistake as soon as the words left my mouth.

"What do you mean? Have you seen her ghost or something?"

I didn't know how to proceed. If I wanted him to confess to any crimes (if he indeed was responsible) I needed to take a different approach, and maybe telling the truth was the right way to go.

"I've seen my grandmother's ghost ever since I returned to town. She's the one who's been saying all along that you were the one responsible for her murder."

"But now this Bobby guy has been arrested?"

"Yes, but she says that there was no way he could have done this by himself. There must be a powerful witch behind him pulling the strings. She thinks you're that witch."

Hunter laughed as he got the bartender's attention and ordered himself another scotch on the rocks. I ordered a Bahama Mama for myself.

"What's so funny?"

"Has your dear grandmother told you about the Witches' Council?"

I nodded.

"I bet she hasn't told you everything about them. Witches aren't supposed to be ghosts. That's the whole point of being a witch: once you die, you're pretty conscious of what's going on."

"Well, she says she doesn't remember what happened at the time of her death. That's why she needed my help before she could move on."

Hunter laughed again. "It all makes sense now," he said and took a sip of his drink.

"What do you mean?"

"It's been your grandmother all along. She's the one that's been pulling the strings."

"That doesn't make any sense..."

"It does if you really think about it. Who has the most to gain with the Crowleys out of the way?"

"Are you still on about that artifact she supposedly stole from you guys?"

"She *did* steal it. But that's beside the point. Your grandmother is not dumb, there's a bigger game she's playing here. If she was a proper witch, she would not be haunting the living right now and manipulating things in the material world. That's one of the things the council frowns upon."

"But the spell I did to find Nathan and Boyd's killer led me right to you..."

"Was your grandmother there when you cast the spell?"

"Yes, but..."

"Not buts, ifs, or ands about it Rory. Your grand-mother manipulated the spellcasting so that it would lead you to me."

"I don't believe you," I said as I got up to go. "My grandmother has been nothing but good to me. She left me her house, her shop. Why would she do all of that?"

"I don't know but I can tell you that it's probably for nothing good."

"You're telling me she killed herself to put all of this in motion? That's crazy."

"She fell down some stairs, didn't she? And didn't Detective Morgan rule her death an accident?"

"Yeah, but Bobby confessed."

"Yes, but you yourself said that he's being manipulated by someone."

"So what are you trying to say?"

"I'm saying that your grandmother's death really was an accident and that she put everything else in motion afterwards."

I finished my Bahama Mama and was out of there in no time.

I didn't even bother saying goodbye to Hunter. I didn't believe a word of what he was saying, but if he was right, Scott was in danger.

TWENTY-FOUR

I PARKED THE BUG IN FRONT OF MY GRANDMOTHER'S house. I looked up at the foreboding house and the dark clouds overhead. The blue moon, the second full moon of the month was clearly visible in one corner of the sky.

To say that my grandmother's house looked unwelcoming would be an understatement. I was sure Hunter was to be blamed for that. He'd said things that made me doubt everything I knew about Rose, and maybe even Rhi.

It didn't make much sense to me and I was determined to get to the bottom of this. I would ask Rose point-blank and see what she had to say on the matter.

I shut the door behind me and almost jumped out of my skin when I saw Rose standing in the hallway.

"Hello granddaughter," she said, and her voice and manner sent shivers down my spine.

It's just your imagination, I told myself. The things Hunter had said ran through my mind and made me doubt everything I had believed about my grandmother, maybe even my whole family.

"Hi," I quickly said as I walked past her. I didn't want her to see the look of fear on my face.

"How did it go? Did Hunter confess?"

"No, of course not. But he did offer an alternative explanation. Where's Scott by the way?"

"Last time I saw him he was up in his room. I think he was packing his things. He told me not to say anything, but..."

"What? Scott is going back to New York?"

"That is what it looks like. But don't worry Rory, he doesn't belong in our world anyway. He's only human."

"We're all human," I said and headed for the stairs.

Rose appeared in front of me out of nowhere.

I took a step back. "I'm really not in the mood for another lecture right now."

"No lectures, Rory. Just a question. What did Hunter have to say for himself?"

"He had a theory," I wasn't sure if this was the smartest idea, but unless I just spilled the beans we'd always have this between us.

"And may I hear this theory?"

"He thinks...well, he thinks that you are the one responsible for all of this."

The look of shock on my grandmother's face could

not have been faked. Either she was shocked because it wasn't true or because I knew.

"Rory, listen to me, this Hunter fellow is dangerous. I do not want you to talk to him again, at least not while you're by yourself."

"So you're saying that he's making all this up?"

"Of course, that shouldn't even be a question. Do you really trust a man you barely know over your own family?"

Rose had a point. Hunter may have been good-looking and mysterious but that didn't mean that he knew what he was talking about.

"I'm sorry. Let's talk about it later. I'm really tired and I'd really like to talk to Scott." That much was true. I headed upstairs and this time Rose let me.

"We'll have plenty of time to talk later," Rose said. "Just think about what I've said. I've always wanted the best for you, Rory."

I was more confused than ever as I made my way upstairs. I didn't know who to believe. All I knew was that I didn't want to see Scott going anywhere.

I knocked on his door and when I heard him yell "Wait!" I immediately opened it.

"Hey!" Scott protested as he tried to hide what he was doing. Rose was right: he was packing. She was at least telling the truth about that, if nothing else.

"Were you going to tell me you were leaving or were you going to just disappear in the middle of the night?"

Scott looked guilty as charged. "Of course I was going to tell you. I was just making sure I was ready before then. I didn't want you to talk me out of it."

"What brought this on?"

"I was talking with your cousin and Rose and they made it pretty clear that I'll do nothing but hold you back."

"What? That's crazy. You're my best friend, why would you be holding me back? That doesn't even make any sense."

"Well, it made sense when they pointed it out. You're a witch, and I'm a mundane. We don't have much in common anymore. Plus, they said I could get in trouble with the Witches' Council if they found out I knew about you guys."

"Scott, I talked to Hunter tonight and a lot of what he was saying is making sense right now."

"What did he say?"

I told Scott about Hunter's suspicions.

"Wow," Scott said. It was clear that he didn't know what to think about my revelation.

"I don't think we should spend the night here," I offered as I looked at his half-filled suitcase. "Maybe you had the right idea after all."

"Are you sure that's necessary? It's not like we have any evidence to prove what he's saying."

"It's just a feeling I have. We could stay at the inn or at the motel or something. Just for tonight."

"Fine," Scott sighed. "If you think it's really necessary."

Scott continued to pack his suitcase.

"I think it'll be a bit suspicious if we both went out tonight with huge suitcases in tow. I was just planning on telling Rose that we're going out for drinks or something."

"Look at you thinking like a sleuth. I'm proud of you, Rory."

"That means the world to me," I said sarcastically.

After we were properly dressed we made our way downstairs. I was surprised to see that Rhi was in the living room.

"What are you doing here?" I asked her. "I mean, I didn't hear you come in," I added when I saw the defeated look on her face.

"Oh, I have a key and Rose said it would be fine. You don't mind, do you?"

"No," I said carefully. "It just took me by surprise. Anyway, Scott and I are going out."

I had my hand on the door-handle when I heard Rhi behind me.

"It's almost midnight," she said. "Where are you two going at this hour?"

"For drinks," Scott quickly said before I had a chance to answer. "It was my idea. I've been feeling pretty claustrophobic in this house."

I tried to open the door but it wouldn't budge. I tried to unlock it but everything was stuck.

"What is this?" I asked Rose and Rhi as I turned around to face them. It seemed that getting out of the house tonight was going to be trickier than I thought.

"It's for your own protection," Rose said as she floated closer to where Scott and I were standing. I couldn't help but feel intimidated and cornered, which I guess was her intent all along. "Hunter Crowley is on the loose as you well know yourself. Let's contact the Witches' Council and have them deal with it."

"Yeah, cousin, listen to grandma. She knows where it's at."

I had the sudden urge to slap that sanctimonious expression from Rhi's face, but I held back.

"I'm an adult, I think I can make my own decisions," I spat back. "Besides, I don't think the Witches' Council would look kindly on the ghost of a witch roaming about. Isn't that right, grandma?"

"You little ungrateful..."

"It's okay, grandma, it seems that the jig is up," Rhi said, and then she turned her gaze on me. "How did you know about the ghost thing anyway?"

"Hunter told me, and it seems he was right."

Scott scooted closer to me as Rhi joined Rose. We were trapped in the house with two witches, one dead and one very much alive, and I had no idea what to do.

There was only one thing I could do: keep them talking.

"Why did you fake your own death?" I asked Rose point-blank.

"It was an unfortunate accident, as the good detective was so keen to point out, but I used it to my advantage."

"And you, Rhi? What's your role in all of this?"

"Besides unlimited power? What else do I need?"

I looked from Rose to Rhi and saw something very similar in both their eyes: the lust for power.

"Why did you leave everything to me? Why did you even want me to return? Wouldn't it have been easier to leave everything to Rhi?" I asked my grandmother.

Rose laughed as she floated around the room. "My dear granddaughter. You really don't get it, do you?"

"Get what?"

"Yeah," Scott added. "This isn't making any sense."

"Shut up, mundane," Rhi spat at Scott and with the flick of her finger, he was flying across the room.

I moved to see if he was alright, but Rose stopped me. Then I saw Scott get up and moan and I breathed in relief.

And then Rhi was by his side, and my heart got caught in my throat.

Rhi put a hand on Scott's shoulder and he froze in place before he could make another move.

"Why are you doing all of this?" I was on the verge of

tears, but I couldn't let them see me like that. I needed to keep my cool, and I had plenty of anger to focus on.

"Stupid girl," Rose said as she flew all around me. It was unnerving not knowing what her next move was and feeling like I was powerless to stop it. "All I've ever wanted was you."

TWENTY-FIVE

"ME? WHAT DO YOU MEAN BY THAT?"

"It's a blue moon, Rory," Rose said as she stopped in front of me and pointed out the window.

"And?"

"You really should have studied the spellbook a little closer. A blue moon is one of the most powerful times for witches. This is the time we do extra big spells, and the one I have planned for you will take a lot out of me and Rhi."

I was still no wiser to what they had planned. "Tell me why you're doing all of this." I was starting to sound like a broken record even to myself.

"I need a body," Rose said and her words sent a shiver down my spine.

"That's why you left everything to me..." It all made sense now.

"Yes, because after I take your body, it will all be mine again. Clever, don't you think?"

"What makes you think I'll agree to it?"

Rose laughed. A screeching laugh that made me think of old, long-forgotten nightmares from my childhood. Now I understood why my mother never wanted me to find out I was a witch.

"If you don't agree, I'm afraid we'll have to kill Scott. You wouldn't like that, would you?"

Rose suddenly poofed out of existence. I quickly went to the aid of Scott.

Then I saw that Rhi had a knife to Scott's throat.

"Don't come any closer," she warned with a crazed look in her eyes.

"Rhi, why are you doing this?" I asked as I tried to buy some time.

"You know why," Rhi spat back. "You're not one of us, Rory, and you never will be. It's better this way."

"Let Scott go and I'll do anything you want."

"I'm not falling for that."

I could see by the look on Scott's face that he was thinking of just kicking Rhi and ending the whole situation, but I could also see the light shining from Rhi's hand. She held him down with magic, not human strength. I signaled Scott to stay calm.

"Rose! Show yourself!" I yelled out. I knew Rhi was just the puppet and that my grandmother was the master pulling all the strings.

Rose poofed into existence again, but this time, she was looking at Rhi, not me.

"Everything is ready," she said to Rhi and disappeared again.

Rhi held the shiny blade closer to Scott's exposed neck.

"Go to the attic, Rory," she hissed.

I hesitated as I slowly climbed the stairs.

"Stop wasting my time, or I'll waste your friend here, understand?"

"I understand," I said as I quickened my pace.

I was in a lose-lose situation. If I tried to fight Rhi, she would kill Scott before I could stop her. But giving into their demands could mean the death of both me and Scott.

Once we were in the attic, Rhi and Scott right on my tail, I decided to ask Rose a question.

"If I agree to do this, how do I know you guys won't kill Scott anyway? He's already seen too much."

Rose smiled and I had the urge to crawl into a hole and hide there forever. "We have a forgetting spell. Your friend won't remember anything that has happened in the last week by the time we're done with him."

"You can do that?"

"Of course. We're witches, remember?"

How could I forget. I looked upon the scene in front of me: Rose was in the middle of a magical circle big enough for two. I did not want to step into that circle.

Everything in my mind told me that that would be the death of me. I needed to devise a plan.

Then I remembered the magic lessons Rhi had given me. I was sure that any big displays of magic would be noticeable, but what about little ones? Rose was preoccupied with the spell that was about to take place, and Rhi had her hands full with Scott.

I noticed that the attic door was open just a crack and smiled. It was now or never. If the cat really was my familiar or helper or whatever, now was the time to make an appearance. I sent a telepathic message across the airways as Rose and Rhi discussed the finer points of the spell that was about to take place.

"The moon will be at its apex in less than half an hour. The spell needs to be in motion by then," Rose was telling Rhi, and me presumably. I myself was focused on stopping the spell.

"What will happen to me after you take over my body?" I asked, trying to stall for time.

"Usually, this spell is done while both parties are still alive," Rose admitted. "The younger soul goes into the older body, but since there is no body to go to in this case, my best guess is that you will dissipate completely or become a ghost."

Neither sounded like a pleasant experience, and I hated the fact that Rose said it so casually like it was the most normal thing in the world.

"Now stop wasting my time and enter the circle,"

Rose said as she held out her hand to me. I looked in Rhi's direction and saw the contorted look of evil on her face as she held the knife to Scott's throat. Poor Scott couldn't even speak. He could barely even move because of Rhi's magic "touch."

Where was that damn cat?

I walked as slow as I could toward Rose, praying for some kind of miracle.

When I heard Rhi's shrieking scream, I knew that it had arrived.

I looked back in her direction and saw that she was sprawled on the floor holding her bloody leg. I saw the cat run as fast as it could out of the attic.

"Damn cat," Rhi hissed. "I knew we should have gotten rid of it."

"I already told you that that cat will be my familiar once I take over Rory's body!" Rose hissed back.

Scott regained his motor functions and ran to my side. He took my hand and we quickly ran out of there, shutting the door in Rhi's face. I didn't bother to lock it or enchant it: Rhi was a witch, too, after all.

Just as we made it to the front door a loud roar of thunder shook the house and I remembered that the door was magically locked.

I turned the handle and it still wouldn't budge.

"Damn!" I hissed.

"Out of my way," Scott said as he pushed me back gently. He used all his strength to smash through the door, but all he ended up with was a very sore shoulder. "It's too strong."

It was a huge wooden door. What was he thinking? Even if it wasn't magicked, I doubted that someone could break through it that easily.

"Let me try something," I said as I looked around but the cat was nowhere in sight.

I tried to remember the unlocking spell that my grandmother had taught me to open the door but the strange words seemed out of reach.

"Did you really think it was going to be that easy?" Rhi hissed as she hopped her way down the stairs.

Loud thumps made my heart almost jump out of my chest. I breathed a sigh of relief when I realized that it was somebody banging on the door.

"Help! In here! Help!" I yelled as loud as I could and Scott joined in.

"Shut the hell up," Rhi said as she lifted her hand. I could see magical energy making its way toward both Scott and I. It split in midair and started to choke us both.

I fell on the floor as I tried to breathe but couldn't. Scott seemed to be having the same problem.

Then something peculiar began to happen. I had a sort of tunnel vision that let a sort of peace overcome me. I saw the potential all around me. I gathered a ball of energy in my hand and sent it in Rhi's direction.

The ball of energy exploded in Rhi's face just like I

wanted it to. She fell backward and her spell broke. I could breathe again. I looked over at Scott and saw the look of relief on his face.

And then the front door flew open and let the howling wind and rain inside the house.

Not to mention the dark foreboding figure that lorded over all of us.

TWENTY-SIX

THE DARK FIGURE STEPPED INTO THE LIGHT. I COULD SEE his hands were flowing with magic.

It was Hunter.

Almost instinctively I ran into his arms.

He held his strong arms around me and told me that everything would be alright.

Scott stepped out of the house as soon as Rhi recovered.

"You!" She hissed in Hunter's direction. "You've ruined everything!"

I saw as she gathered a large ball of energy and spelled it with words I could not understand. The hatred in her eyes was palatable.

Hunter quickly took my hand in his and told me to repeat after him.

I lent him my energy and my voice as I repeated the

strange words over and over in unison with his own voice. He held out his other hand in a defensive position.

I could see a field of sorts or a shield of energy forming in front of us. Rhi was too angry to notice. She threw the ball of energy in our direction, uttering words of destruction if I had to guess.

The shield did its job and the ball of energy bounced back to its sender.

Rhi flew back across the room and once she hit the floor she was out cold. There was a trickle of blood on her forehead where she had hit a table.

I breathed a sigh of relief.

"It's finally over," I said. "Thank you, thank you," I kept repeating to Hunter.

"You imbeciles!" I heard my grandmother's familiar voice as she materialized right in front of us. "You've ruined everything." She looked down on Rhi's unconscious form. "Stupid girl," I heard her whisper.

"Stay away, you old hag," Hunter hissed in Rose's direction.

"And what will you do to stop me?" She challenged him as she stood mere feet from us.

She flew in closer and glared at Hunter. "You are nothing compared to me, boy."

"That might have been true when you were alive, but that's no longer the case." Hunter took out a silver amulet from his pocket and held it out in front of him like a priest would a crucifix when faced with a vampire in those cheesy horror movies.

"What is the meaning of this?" Rose asked, her eyes suddenly filled with fear.

"It's time for you to go, old hag," he said and then proceeded to chant strange words.

Rose's ghostly form coalesced and formed into mist which in turn entered the amulet. Hunter quickly took out a small box from his other pocket and put the amulet inside.

"That should keep her safe for now," he said.

"Keep who safe?" a familiar voice asked.

Detective Jack Morgan stepped in from the shadows and the rain, which had miraculously stopped as soon as Hunter broke through the door.

"It took you long enough, detective," Hunter said.

"You called him?" I whispered to Hunter as we all went inside the house.

"Of course, I didn't want to take any chances. Bobby was just a regular human if you remember, and he almost killed you."

"You have a point there," I said.

"Are you okay?" I asked Scott when he closed the door after us.

"I will be," was all he said with a sad expression on his face. I made a mental note that we would finally have that conversation about him leaving, but right now we had more pressing matters to deal with.

"What happened here?" Jack asked as he looked down on Rhi's unconscious form.

"It's a long story," I quickly said.

Jack turned around and smiled that sad smile of his. "I've got plenty of time."

I told him that Rhi had attacked me and tried to kill me.

"Why would she do that?" Jack asked.

"I guess she was angry that our grandmother left me the house and shop." I was proud of myself for being so quick to come up with a plausible lie.

"That makes sense. So are you saying that she talked Bobby into trying the same?"

"I guess. I can't say she was very talkative. She had a knife in her hand and she seemed pretty determined to catch me. Thankfully Hunter arrived in the nick of time."

"You've certainly got excellent timing, Mr. Crowley."

Hunter smiled in the detective's direction. It was clear the two men didn't like each other very much. Jack seemed suspicious of Hunter, and he had good reason to be. But it was not my place to enlighten the detective about the magical world.

"And you detective arrived right when everything was over. Isn't that some kind of cliché about cops?"

The look of anger on Jack's face was unmistakable.

Before the two men could start a fight, I stepped in between them.

"Could you please restrain her before she comes to?" I asked Jack nicely.

He took out his handcuffs and did just that. I heard a low moan escape Rhi's lips.

"I'll call her an ambulance just in case," he said.

I nodded.

I pulled Hunter aside and let Scott watch over Rhi while I got some questions out of the way.

"What happens when she wakes? What if she uses magic to escape?"

"She won't be using magic for quite some time. That spell I bounced back on her made sure of that. But I did contact the Witches' Council just in case. They're aware of the situation and they'll be in town tomorrow to transfer her to a witch prison out of state."

"That sounds ludicrous," I said. "First witch police, now a witch prison? What else don't I know about?"

Hunter smiled that mysterious and devilish smile of his. "Plenty," was all he said.

"What about Carver? Isn't he a witch, too?"

Hunter looked crestfallen. "Yes," he said. "I knew as soon as I contacted the council that there was a chance that they would take Carver away as well."

"I'm so sorry Hunter," I honestly said. "I'm sorry I put you in that position."

"Don't worry about it. Carver made his choices. A

witch prison is the safest place for him. If he even tried to expose magic to the mundanes, the consequences would have been much worse."

Jack joined us as we heard sirens in the distance.

"I'll let you guys rest. Make sure to stop by the station to make statements."

I nodded and thanked the detective. I watched as the EMT's wheeled out Rhi's semi-unconscious body.

"That was freaking crazy," Scott said when it was just him, Hunter and me in the house.

Hunter nodded. "It was certainly ballsy. I haven't heard of witches behaving this badly since my last run in with your grandmother. I guess there's just something about the Wiltz women..."

"Hey! That's not very nice!" I gently punched Hunter in the shoulder and was surprised at how solid he felt. He definitely worked out, there was no doubt about it.

Hunter laughed and Scott joined him.

"Too soon?" Hunter asked.

"Way too soon," Scott said and I agreed.

TWENTY-SEVEN

Scott went up to rest and I told him that I'd soon be joining him. Hunter and I made our way up to the attic so that he could see what my grandmother and cousin had in store for me.

"Wow," he said when he looked at the setup and the spell in the book. "This is some dark magic."

"What'll happen to her?" I asked him.

"Your cousin or your grandmother?"

"My grandmother."

"I'll hand this little amulet with her soul in it to the Witches' Council and I guess they'll have to decide."

Meow. I turned to see the cat walking in elegantly like it owned the place. I had completely forgotten. I took the cat in my hands and hugged it.

"Thank you so much little one," I whispered in its ear.

All I got was another *meow* in response. Then the cat practically jumped out of my hands and ran away.

"I see you've found your familiar."

I nodded. "So they were telling the truth about that at least?"

"Yeah, all witches have helpers."

"What's yours?"

"A raven."

"You have a raven as a pet?"

Hunter laughed. "Gods no. He comes and goes as he pleases."

"My cat is the same. I don't even know its name yet. I'm pretty sure it's a he, though."

"It'll reveal its name to you when it's ready, and then you'll be able to call upon it whenever you want."

It was nice to be talking to another witch about all this stuff. Especially now that my cousin was in custody and my grandmother's ghost was headed to God knows where.

"It's late. I better be going. I have to give Carver a visit and explain the situation to him. I don't think his sentence will be as long as your cousin's, though, thankfully."

"Good luck," I said and smiled. "Thank you so much."

"Don't mention it," Hunter said as we headed downstairs.

"If you ever need anything," I offered and then realized how it sounded.

Once we were at the front door Hunter turned back to face me. He had that devilish grin almost playing across his lips but then it was gone as soon as it appeared.

"There *is* something you could do for me."

"HERE IT IS," I said the next day. We had decided that we all needed a good night's sleep after yesterday's events.

Hunter took the artifact in his hands. He was immediately come over with emotion. It was the first time I had seen him close to tears. It was quite the sight. He recovered pretty quickly and his lips curved up into a smile instead of a frown.

"You don't know how happy my folks will be when I come home with this."

"Hopefully it softens the blow about the situation with Carver."

"Yeah, I'm definitely preparing myself for some drama."

"So are you leaving town for good?" The question sounded sadder than I wanted it to, but it was true: I liked Hunter and I hated to see him go.

"Don't worry, Rory," Hunter said and laughed at his own rhyme. "I bought back our old house. I'm going to be living across the street from you again."

"What makes you think I'm staying in town?" I teased him.

"You've got a shop to run, don't you? Who else will cater to Hazelville's magical and not-so-magical community?"

"I guess you have a point there."

We said our goodbyes and I watched as Hunter rode away on his motorcycle. I hoped to see him again sooner rather than later. All this witch stuff was new to me, and Hunter was the only witch I knew now.

"Did you guys set a date?" Scott asked as he emerged from the book area with a book in his hands.

"Don't be ridiculous, Scott," I said. And then more seriously: "We need to talk."

"I know what this is about," he said as he smartly put the book he was leafing through on the counter. "Lay it on me, sister."

"I don't think you should go back to New York. I think you should stay here with me."

Scott sighed and ran a hand through his dark blond locks, which had gotten longer than usual.

"I don't know, Rory. You know I love you, but I don't think there's anything here for me. Hazelville is such a small town, and if I want to be a writer…"

"It's the perfect place to be. Be inspired, Scott, what are you waiting for?"

Scott groaned at my enthusiasm and I can't say I blamed him.

"Think about it. You can help me around the shop or you can put in an application at the local newspaper. I bet once they see New York on your resume they'll hire you on the spot! And if they don't, I could always cast a spell or something."

Scott laughed. A good hearty laugh that told me that everything would be okay after all.

"I'll give it a shot," he said. "But I'm not making any promises."

"That's all I'm asking."

BOOK & Candle felt emptier and lonelier than usual. Scott was in the back room trying to make sense of the computer system that I had barely an idea how to run. I guess I should have listened better when Rhi tried to explain all of it to me. Scott said that I might need to talk to a lawyer, and that was something I definitely wasn't looking forward to.

I saw two figures out of the corner of my eye and got excited by the prospect that we actually had some customers coming to our store.

It wasn't customers. The two figures entering the shop weren't even alive. They did not need to open the door: they just walked right through it.

"Nathan, Boyd, what are you guys doing here?" I asked genuinely surprised to see them. I thought they would move on now that their killer was caught.

"Unfinished business," Nathan said as he stood on the other side of the counter. Boyd joined his friend and nodded.

When Hunter had trapped my grandmother in that amulet I thought that was the last time I'd have to deal with ghosts. Apparently I'd been wrong.

"What kind of unfinished business?"

"We came to apologize," Nathan said.

"Yeah," Boyd said, looking away in embarrassment. It was interesting seeing the two youths acting so proper.

"What are you sorry for? Throwing a rock through my window is nothing compared to what my cousin and grandmother did to me."

Nathan nodded. "I knew they were bad news the moment they came to us. Well, Rhiannon came to us first and gave us some money to throw a rock through your window. Then she tried to hire us to attack you."

"What?"

"Yeah, she said that she just wanted us to scare you, but that seemed like too much to us. Besides, there was no way we wouldn't have gotten caught."

So that was Rhi's plan all along. "What happened when you refused?"

"You know what happened," Boyd said and I realized my mistake. Of course I knew what happened.

"She convinced Bobby to cut your breaks," I said out loud.

"Yes, and the worst part was when we died we became ghosts and then your grandmother came and paid us a visit. She told us that our families were going to pay if we told you anything."

"That's why you guys were so reluctant to talk to me and Scott. That makes sense. But I do have one question."

"Shoot," Boyd said.

"I saw a magic bag in front of your mother's house," I told Nathan. "How did it get there?"

"Your cousin left it there after I died. She told me that it would let her hurt my mother if I spoke about what happened."

"I guess I'll have to pay a visit to your neighborhood again."

Nathan nodded. "Thank you. At first, I thought all witches were evil, but you're different, aren't you?"

"I certainly hope so."

"Well, we should be on our way," Nathan said. He smiled as he turned to go.

"Bye," Boyd said shyly as he followed his friend.

"Wait," I called after them as I followed them outside the shop. Thankfully there were few people on the sidewalk, and even if there were, I didn't really care. I had already earned a reputation around town.

The two youths turned back.

"Where will you guys go from here?"

"I don't know," Nathan said. "But I do feel a pull.

We're fading away from this world. It's time for us to join the other side, wherever that might be."

"Good luck," I said.

"You too," the two youths said in unison as they faded out of existence.

"Who were you talking to?" Jack asked as he looked in the direction where the two youths had disappeared.

"Friends," I said. I was surprised to see Jack up and about, but he was the only law enforcement in town.

He wore very fine fitting jeans and a leather jacket. He looked like a cliché, but a very good-looking one.

Jack looked at me like I had lost it.

"Is there something you wanted to see me about, detective?"

Jack frowned. "I told you to call me Jack."

I smiled my warmest smile, no hint of sarcasm in it at all, or so I hoped. "What is it you wanted to talk to me about, Jack?" I tried again.

This time the detective smiled as he followed me into the air-conditioned bliss of the shop.

"I've just come to check on you guys. A lot's happened in the last week or so."

"Aren't you nice? I can't say I'm over any of it yet, but I'm getting there. Honestly, I'm still in shock that my own cousin would try to murder me."

"Yeah," Jack said, though he didn't seem entirely convinced by my story. "It's strange how all of that played out, isn't it?"

"I guess," I said noncommittally. "I'm just glad it all worked out in the end. Thanks to you and Hunter."

"I'm afraid Mr. Crowley is the one who helped the most. The sheriff wasn't happy when he heard about what happened."

"Oh?"

"He's a strange fellow. He kept on insisting that we'd gotten something wrong. Either way, it was all over when your cousin was transferred out of our jurisdiction. In fact, the same thing happened with Carver Crowley. Do you have any idea how that happened?"

"No. Why would I?"

"It was just a hunch."

"Can I get you something to drink? Are you interested in a spell candle or maybe even a book on the occult arts?" I knew I sounded like I was telling him to blow off, and in a way that was exactly what I was doing. I wasn't in the mood to be accused of things, even if the accusations weren't entirely unfounded.

"I see. I'll be on my way, Ms. Wiltz. Have a nice day."

"Have a nice day, detective," I said, this time keeping all the warmth out of my voice.

I watched as Jack walked out of my shop.

"Well that went bad pretty quick," Scott said when he joined me by the counter.

"Well, you can't say I didn't try," I said coldly.

Scott smiled. "Don't worry, I don't think you were the

one in the wrong here. You've just been through a traumatic experience and here he is trying to berate you."

"Thanks, Scott," I said honestly. Finally, someone who understood.

"You ready to go home?"

Was it really time to close up already? I looked up at the clock and saw that it was five to six. It indeed was the time.

"Yeah," I agreed. "Let's go home."

68731877R00147

Made in the USA
Lexington, KY
18 October 2017